MUDDY BITES

JESSICA TASTET

DANDELION WISH
Publications

MUDDY BITES

A Raleigh Cheramie Mystery

By
Jessica Tastet

Dandelion Wish Publications

Muddy Bites

Copyright May 2020 Jessica Tastet

Cover Design by Ashley Comeaux-Foret

ISBN 978-0-9986173-7-4

ISBN 978-0-9986173-8-1

ONE

Raleigh Cheramie slurped down the smooth frothiness that had been a Bayou Mudslide and slid the glass toward the middle of the weathered tabletop. Donnie had been correct when he said she'd love their new chocolate sauce. As the longtime bartender at Roxy's, he knew just how she liked her alcohol—disguised by chocolate.

"Earth to Raleigh," Sheri said, snapping her fingers at her from across the table. "Are you even listening?"

"Uh-hmm." Raleigh nodded, licking the last bit of sauce from her lips. "Party, guests, details, etc."

"No." Sheri frowned, her blue eye shadow crinkling at the corners. "Madison's late again."

Mike tapped an empty beer mug on the table and grinned. "Well, she is late to plan the anniversary party."

Raleigh nodded, grateful for his arbitration and said, "Madison will be late to her own funeral, and if there was a chance of getting her down the aisle, she'd be late to her own wedding as well. We'd think something wrong with her if she showed up on time."

Raleigh wasn't worried—yet.

Looking around the bar, she noticed Roxy's Thursday nights

regulars had grown younger. On the dance floor, the small group looked like teens with their distressed jeans and layered tops and leather bracelets. Barbeaux had more than its fair share of bars for a small town, so Raleigh's group could go to Doug's bar or Phil's. Even The Seafood Camp may have a good happy hour crowd, but Roxy's was where Mike had been coming since he'd returned to Barbeaux. He'd be hesitant to make the change.

Sheri sipped from her pink cocktail, cherry still soaking at the bottom. "I have it on reliable town gossip that Madison has turned quite punctual these days with her new business."

Raleigh's younger sister Madison had been irresponsible much of her life, and after a few recent personal mishaps, she'd attempted to get her life in order with a new special events dating service. In true Madison fashion, she had to do it big and bold and, Raleigh could only hope, legal.

"She'll get here to plan the party," Mike said, frowning as he did his own sweep of the bar. "Can you imagine being married for sixty-three years?"

Raleigh grimaced. Sixty-three years was a foreign concept to her. She hadn't been able to keep her last relationship going six months, and now Mike said they needed to give it some time to make sure she didn't want him as some rebound relationship. She didn't even know what that meant. How much time did you give it before you realized it wasn't happening?

"Me'Maw says the secret is to have a sense of humor," Raleigh said, wiping some chocolate sauce off the rim of the glass with her finger. "One has to have the ability to laugh at Paw's hard head."

Mike chuckled, his blond hair rustling as he shook his head. "And dance. That woman loves to dance with the old man. We must have music at this surprise party."

A loud screech pierced the rumble of chatter and blaring music from the direction of the dance floor, and all three of them turned to see its origin.

Heading toward the exit from the dance floor, a young t-shirted man twisted the wrist of a girl as she tried to walk away from him. Squinting to see through the hazy smoke and dim lights, Raleigh recognized a streaky blonde chunk of hair through the brown braid falling over the young woman's shoulder.

Mike rose from his barstool. "Is that Emma?"

Raleigh followed Mike to the dance floor group, recognizing the faces of the small group on the dance floor as six of the high school students in the journalism class that she and Mike had volunteered a few weeks ago to mentor. While working to get a newspaper program started as a community outreach program, Raleigh hadn't discussed much about the students' personal life, but she knew enough to know that the only way they had made it into the bar was with fake IDs, or Donnie had gone senile. At only twenty-six that was unlikely. Roxy and his dad ran a tight ship and would break his fingers one by one if they caught him serving alcohol to a minor. His father was old school with this bar, and Roxy could be a little rough around the edges. But this was her place, and she wouldn't risk underage drinking.

Jeremy twisted Emma's arm and yanked her toward him as Mike reached the edge of the group.

Mike nodded hello and then said, "What are y'all doing here?"

"Mr. Simmons?" Olivia's eyes widened and then darted toward the door.Raleigh glared at Jeremy's tight grip on Emma's arm. "We didn't imagine seeing you all in a place like this."

"Dancing." Caleb swallowed, his Adams apple bobbing. "We just wanted to dance. No harm done."

Raleigh looked directly into Emma's watery eyes. "Everything okay here?"

"Everything is fine, Miss," Jeremy said. "No trouble here."

"If you don't mind, I'd like to hear if from Emma." Raleigh maintained eye contact with Emma, whose eyes shifted around the group, not wanting to maintain contact with Raleigh. In class, Emma had exhibited a bubbly personality with an unfailing smile. Tonight, she appeared nervous, unable to pull away from Jeremy's grip, and unable to look at Raleigh and Mike as the red outline of Jeremy's fingerprints formed on her bare arm.

Jeremy's bony chest puffed up. "What the hell you think is going on? We aren't in the classroom if you missed it, Ms. C. This is a barroom." He offered a forced laugh. "Nice place for a teacher to hang out though. Great role models you two are."

Mike stepped closer to Raleigh, who stood across from the two teenage lovebirds. "Calm down, Jeremy." Mike had hung back, waiting to see what unfolded. He always played observer first, while Raleigh's game plan always involved rushing in and allowing it to slam her in the face.

Jeremy faked laugh again. "I am calm. I don't need you two. We'll get out of here before you become snitches and rat us out or something." Jeremy yanked his head in the direction of the others. "Funny how you two try to act cool and shit in class, but you're just as out of touch as the rest of them."

Jeremy pulled Emma by her arm as he stalked toward the exit.

"Emma," Raleigh called out, "do you need a ride?"

Emma looked back, her lips twitching. "I will be okay, Ms. C."

The others followed them out the door. The red-haired, penciled-in eyebrow girl from the second desk stopped and patted Raleigh on the shoulders. "Don't worry. Jeremy's just a hot head, but he'll calm down in five minutes."

"Look after her Olivia," Mike said, nodding at Caleb and the other two boys that Raleigh always confused. One was Seth and the other was Ethan. Raleigh could never get their names straight as they both had dark hair, brown eyes, and stood at 5'10".

Raleigh watched the door swing closed behind them. "Do you think we should go after them?" An uneasy feeling swirled in the pit of her stomach, and she was certain it wasn't the Mudslide or the new chocolate sauce swirling in there.

"Nah." Mike shook his head as he turned back toward the interior of the bar. "They won't listen to us. Do you remember what it was like being sixteen?"

Raleigh cringed. "Yep."

Sheri watched as they returned to their table. She shook her head with a smile on her face.

"Donnie and I had a chat about the young crowd in this bar lately," Sheri said before tipping her glass back against her lips.

Mike nodded as Donnie cleared the glasses from their table. "Next time you may want to confiscate those fake IDs."

Donnie looked at the door, a frown twisting on his full lips. "I thought something looked off about the plastic." He shook his head. "Thursday nights are the worse, you know?"

Raleigh's cellphone buzzed on the bar. She glanced down at the screen and saw Madison Cheramie flash on the glass.

"Uh-oh." She uttered, frowning at the name. Madison never called. She only texted.

"I'm having the worst night," Madison exclaimed. "Is Mike still with you?"

"Of course, Madison." Raleigh tapped her fingers on the bar. "We've been waiting for you for an hour."

Truthfully, Raleigh didn't know how long they'd been waiting, but she tried to hold her sister accountable for some of her behaviors. Otherwise, she might slip back into the days of dancing on bars and providing illegal services at illicit parties. Someone had to keep her on track.

"I know." Madison blew out air over the phone. "I have a flat tire. Do you know how to change a tire? Because I can't even figure out what end of the tool I'm supposed to use."

A tinge of guilty conscience tugged at her. She may need to start offering Madison the benefit of the doubt. "Where are you?"

"I'm on that stretch of highway near the canal, right before the bridge."

Madison's voice was distant as if a big expanse absorbed it. She must be standing outside of the car on a stretch of highway that contained trees and few passersby.

Raleigh motioned to Mike, and he perked up with raised eyebrows. "Mike and I are on our way."

She briefly explained the situation as she slapped a ten-dollar bill on the counter for Donnie, and they gave Sheri hurried good-byes with promises to reconvene the party planning meeting.

Moments later she slid into the Jeep's passenger seat, pulled her bag from the floorboard, and retrieved the sweater she'd stuffed in there earlier.

Shrugging into the sweater, she glanced toward Mike as he started the engine. "Ever notice how you are always rescuing a Cheramie sister?"

Mike chuckled. "You two do seem to get into plenty messes. I can't say it's all bad playing the hero though."

Raleigh laughed. "Hero, huh?" At first sight, Mike didn't strike anyone as a hero with his shaggy blond hair and tall, lanky build. As the quiet observant type, he was more of a rock; the one there waiting in a crisis to offer strength. The kind of man like her paw. As she waited in angst to see what their next step in this relationship dance was going to be, she noticed the similarities between the two—both men she counted on to be there at all levels of life crisis.

Ten minutes later, the Jeep's headlights illuminated Madison's compact silver coupe on the side of the deserted back road. Mike U-turned in the middle of the road and eased the Jeep into park behind the car's bumper. Madison's car door opened, and she walked to the back to meet them at the trunk of the car.

Madison huffed as she opened the trunk. "You would think that if a car is only a few months old, you could rely on it not getting a flat tire."

"You may have picked up a nail." Mike searched the trunk, his hand feeling around the black carpet. "Getting the spare tire out of these new cars is as difficult as changing it."

Returning to the Jeep, Raleigh shuffled through items in the glove compartment until she clasped down on a small black metal flashlight. Returning to Mike and Madison, she shined the beam of light to create more light and to aid the dim glow of the trunk light. Mike finally found the indentation to lift up the compartment to reach the spare tire.

Madison jogged in place for warmth, her thin white blouse offering little protection against the cool night air. "Dad wants to know if you want to go in together for Mom's birthday gift."

For a moment, Raleigh was taken aback and had to recall her mother's upcoming birthday. Recently, she'd been so focused on her impending thirtieth birthday in April that she hadn't given anyone else's birthday much thought. Not to mention, she let Madison handle her parents, and she handled their grandparents. Divide and conquer seemed the best tactic when her parents didn't really express warm thoughts about having her in the neighborhood permanently.

"Sounds good," Raleigh said, as a rustling of leaves and branches came from the thick underbrush of a mess of foliage and pine trees five feet beyond the passenger doors. She flashed the light in the direction and only caught the slight swaying of thorny leaves.

Mike fiddled in the trunk. "I'm sure it's a coon or something."

Madison laughed nervously. "Maybe we could wait in the Jeep?"

Mike grunted as he pulled the spare tire to the edge of the trunk. He appeared focused on the tire, ignoring Madison's typical selfish comment. "Raleigh, I have a jack in the back of the Jeep."

Handing the flashlight off to Madison, Raleigh walked around to the back of the Jeep to retrieve the jack. Not a single vehicle had driven along this stretch of the highway since they'd pulled off here. Madison could have been stranded out here for hours if her phone battery had been dead, which was pretty common these days. Her sister had a knack for running the battery down and not having a charger handy. As she opened the small door, a static electricity charge jolted through her. Reaching out with her arm, Raleigh steadied herself against the door, but the feeling did not return. Internally, the sharpness subsided, leaving only adrenaline surging in its wake as recognition occurred.

Somewhere, something was happening.

Nothing happened again though. She looked around the wilderness of the area with its overgrown brush, the towering pine trees, and the smell of decaying foliage and it all felt sharper. Her senses reaching out, waiting for what was to come.

Because as Traiteur to the dead, someone had buzzed momentarily into the part of her brain that lay empty, waiting for their last moments on earth to visit her. She could have seconds, minutes, or hours.

Raleigh grabbed the car jack stuffed in the right corner next to a box of ceramic tile that must have been left over from his side hustle and then slammed the door closed.

Handing the jack to Mike, who barely glanced up as he began working on the tire, Raleigh leaned against the front of the Jeep and waited.

Madison jabbered on about some party that was proving a nightmare to plan, and Raleigh went in and out with her attention, her anxiety growing as each minute ticked by.

Thirty minutes later, while Raleigh watched Mike lower the flat tire into the trunk, the dark spots grew in her eyes until nothing but blackness remained.

Moments ticked by. Her eyelids felt droopy, difficult to keep open. Blinking against the heaviness and the blurriness, she began to feel the weight of water pushing at her. Raleigh fought to inhale as the realization that she was submerged in water crushed against her like a wind tunnel. With sharp turns of her head to either side, she noticed long blades of grass swirling in the water, and she could feel nibbles, sharp teeth gnawing at her side.

A silvery orb of light broke through her blurriness from the water surface. The moon. Her hand longed to reach up toward the iridescent shine, for she felt if she could just lift her arm, she could break the surface of the water. Long hair floated, fanning her face, mixing with the brown of the blades of grass dancing to the lapping water.

Brown hair with a touch of blonde.

With a painful inhale from deep in her lower abdominal, Raleigh emerged slumped against the front of the Jeep. Through slow shallow breaths, she attempted to calm her racing pulse. She hated dirty, muddy water. Why did it always have to be water? Mike's arm held gingerly onto her elbow, standing near enough to catch her if she fell from the journey to the dead's last moments. She'd grown better at not damaging her own body when she left it behind to experience the newly departed's last few moments, but it still hadn't become an easy journey in any respect.

Mike's eyes were soft with concerned. "Where are we going?"

Raleigh swallowed against the panic rising in her esophagus. "I couldn't tell where she was."

TWO

The lights of the indiscrete police station cast odd shadows across the few squad and unmarked detective cars across the parking lot. The Jeep's circle headlights illuminated the white brick wall before Mike shut the engine. At this late hour, the Barbeaux Bayou station would be deserted.

Looking at the glass door with its light peeking through the darkness of the hour, Raleigh muttered, "I should have an office here."

From across the center console, Mike squeezed her hand and then released it. "Sheriff Breaux would need to be six feet under first." He offered her a weak lopsided grin, his usual dimple forming to soften his words.

Raleigh sighed. "It's an election year."

Mike widened his eyes and arched his eyebrows to express how ridiculous she was being, a look he'd perfected somewhere back in junior high when puberty had hit. "He's been sheriff for eleven years."

Raleigh gritted her teeth and swung the door open. "It's time for new blood."

Sheriff Breaux had made his name in the papers during the investigation into Ross Blanch's death. He'd made friends with the royal rich folks of Barbeaux and had propelled himself into the sheriff slot when the long-time sheriff of 28 years had retired. With the investigation of Ross's death, Breaux had dragged Raleigh through the mud, poisoning the town against her even though she'd killed him in self-defense. The animosity between the two had originated then because Breaux had been unable to have charges brought by the DA, although he'd made promises to some pretty powerful families.

Inside the lobby door, Tyler leaned back in his chair with his feet propped up on the desk. His eyes were closed until the bell dinged their entrance. From behind, Cousin Joey lumbered out from his desk.

"I got this, Tyler," Joey said, tapping him on the shoulder.

Tyler nodded, watching them leerily. Raleigh didn't blame him. She had yelled at him more than once, embarrassing him like all get out.

In fact, her reputation at the station was *persona non grata*. No one risked working with her due to Sheriff Breaux's orders to stay away from her. After losing her ally, AKA the ex-boyfriend, no one would risk stoking the ire of Sheriff Breaux. She'd called Joey to the rescue to meet them down at the station, knowing that she'd need someone willing to help.

Joey buzzed them in through the newly installed security door and motioned for them to follow him. "So, we got another one?"

Joey had passed his detective's test a year ago and had been waiting for the sheriff to promote him and give him an opportunity without holding his Cheramie connection over his head since then. Finally, he'd been promoted and received a desk with a probationary period to prove himself.

"I don't recognize the location." Raleigh felt the girl within that space in her brain that the dead claimed. Most of the time, it felt like an airy, empty space except when the dead sought out her traiteur abilities. "I've never been there before."

"Let's see if we can't figure it out from the details." Joey turned and looked over the empty desks. "Tyler, can you pull that white board over here for me?"

Tyler jumped up from his chair, his boot banging against the metal desk. After Raleigh had embarrassed him in this station with references to her babysitting services when they were both younger, she knew he feared her, or at the very least, she made him jumpy. She did regret her behavior often, but sometimes she needed to keep the Barbeaux officers on their toes, so they'd be a little more helpful. From behind a ficus tree, Tyler moved the white board to Joey's area, and then he stood expectantly behind, waiting.

Joey placed his hands on his hips in his typical fashion. "Now, let's see what details you can remember."

"Water." Raleigh shuddered. Even with her working on that pesky water phobia, the water deaths still hit her hard. "Shallow water though. I felt as if I picked my head up, I would be above the surface."

Joey nodded toward Tyler who began writing it down on the marker board. Tyler's handwriting looked like a seven-year-old's handwriting lesson, and no one commented when he misspelled shallow.

"What about beneath you?" Mike asked, staring at the board, his eyes narrowed. "Did you get a feel for the bottom surface? Dirt? Sand? Gravel?"

Raleigh closed her eyes again and felt her head against the edge, her fingertips brushing the bottom. Slimy and bumpy. "Mud. Grass growing around me. Long blades that reach out of the water. Thick. Not lilies like the bayou though. Some kind of plant, maybe?"

Joey rubbed his balding head, as he puzzled intently over the details.

A movement from one of the offices caused the small group to turn toward the open door. Detective Max Pyles stood in the doorway, looking his usual disheveled handsome self with his shirt untucked and that dark chick of hair sticking up on the left. His gray eyes slid over Raleigh's at the same speed as the others, not stopping to linger over the ex, she supposed. Then he disappeared into his office. Since their breakup she hadn't had any connections to murder victims, thankfully. She'd helped Joey with a cold case, and there had been the occasional natural death, but really the last three weeks had been quite uneventful. While at the station for the last cold case, Raleigh had experienced a taste of Max's coldness, and she knew he wouldn't be aiding any further in her investigations. Barbeaux Bayou had three detectives counting Joey, and she'd alienated two of them by ending a relationship with one and killing the other one's cousin in self-defense.

Joey cleared his throat, his attention returning to the board. "In South Louisiana that particular water environment could be anywhere. We need something specific to the area. Was there anything else in the water? A structure, maybe?"

Raleigh scrunched up her face in concentration. Typically, she searched for markers, but water caused panic and made it difficult to concentrate when fear drummed through her instead of awareness. She may have missed something that could have led her to the girl while she was dwelling on the gurgling fear crawling through her with dirty water.

With the long hair, she was certain the victim was female. She clung to the space in Raleigh's head in uncertainty and fear and the makings of someone young. Raleigh bore down on the darkness behind her eyelids, trying to see what had been beyond the swimming hair and the water bubbling on her fingertips.

"A cage?" Raleigh grasped at a faint glimpse just beyond the distance of the opalescent fingertips. Wires and squares blurred. "Rectangular, standing up out of the water."

"Crawfish traps?" Mike snapped his fingers in the air. "It's a crawfish pond."

Tyler's hand shook as he wrote this down on the board. The anxiety had caught on, and he waited eagerly in his youth for the next detail.

Joey ran his fingers through his hair. "I can list about ten people right off that have crawfish ponds. We can't go and search every pond in the area."

Pete Sonier strolled in, latching his fingers through the belt loops of his uniformed pants. When he saw the white board, he rocked back and forth on his shoes as he read through the list. "What's going on here?"

Joey gave him the run down while Raleigh focused on remembering any detail that would offer a location. With these sparse details, Raleigh wouldn't be able to find her, and she'd sit unsettled in the empty space in her brain, reminding her that she hadn't fulfilled her duty. Raleigh didn't know how long the dead could stay with her as she'd always been able to find them before now. She'd either been to the place before or she could recognize a reference point. Urgency began to pulse through her.

"Perhaps it's something you heard?" Pete said, looking toward Raleigh. "I know Jordy Pitre's ponds are near the city sewer, and it puts out a droning hum. He doesn't notice it anymore, but when I'm back there, it's all I can focus on."

Joey looked at her expectantly.

Raleigh closed her eyes. Through the water, sound was dulled, as if it came from miles away with a wall between her and the noise. The dirty water edge was within inches of her again. Wait. The surface had rippled, waves moving outward. Right before the movement a boom had sounded in the distance. Then howling erupted in the distance. Dogs.

Raleigh's eyes flew open to the expectant men staring at her. "Dogs and a cannon?"

Mike frowned. "A cannon. As in cannon fire?"

Raleigh rubbed her finger over her scar on her wrist as she puzzled over the sound. "The sound was loud enough to cause the water to ripple."

"They're called sonic cannons," Pete said, nodding. "They are supposed to scare the birds away. I don't know any crawfish farmers who use those though."

Tyler wrote down "sonic cannons" and "dogs" and turned back to the group, waiting.

"What's going on in here?" A voice boomed from a doorway to the left.

Sheriff Breaux filled the doorway, his buttons stretching the fabric of his dress shirt to reveal the black undershirt beneath. A deep scowl was etched across his forehead as he peered intently at Raleigh. "I thought I made myself clear that the only way that I wanted Raleigh Cheramie in my station was in handcuffs."

Max appeared in his own doorway. His arms were crossed, and his face held no expression.

Joey motioned to the board. He hadn't flinched at the volume. "We're working on a missing person's case, sir."

"And let me guess," the sheriff said, shaking his head. "No one has reported this person missing yet?"

No one responded to his question. Tyler remained focused on his boot as he gripped the marker tightly. Mike looked uncomfortable, but Raleigh couldn't blame him considering how often he'd been held for interrogation in the last six months.

"That's what I thought." Sheriff Breaux smiled, his eyes remaining cold. "We are no longer wasting valuable resources on this nonsense. Get her out of my station."

"There's a young girl out there whose family will want to know what happened to her. What are you going to tell them when they ask you why you didn't find her sooner?" Raleigh said, anger pushing out her words. "That you didn't want to listen to the person who tried to help because of your own personal vendetta?"

Sheriff Breaux glared down at her. "I would be real happy to take your confession if that's what you are offering, Ms. Cheramie. Otherwise, ain't nothing you got to say will hold any water in this here station."

Shutting his door, Max disappeared into his office again, relaying the message once again that he would not be offering assistance.

The sheriff chuckled. "Get on home Joey before you and I have a problem. I'd hate to have to demote you for insubordination before you even get a chance to prove you're more than a Cheramie. And Tyler, I'd get back to desk duty if I were you."

Sheriff Breaux returned to his office, and a moment later the blind to the window of his office opened so that he'd have a full view of the floor.

Damn small towns could hold a grudge like nobody's business.

Joey's boot kicked the leg of his desk. He hung his head as he paced, clearly aggravated with the situation and threats.

Raleigh felt panic rise in her head. The girl clenched down tightly, worried she'd go unfound. "I can't just let it go."

"I know," Joey said, looking back at the sheriff's window where he watched them from his desk. "I'm going to keep working on it. I'll make some calls to try and narrow down our pond. In the meantime, you see if there are any other details that will help give us a more specific location."

Raleigh nodded.

As she and Mike left the station with a very subdued staff, Raleigh didn't feel well. The girl's nerves were making her nauseous, and Raleigh couldn't imagine going home and sleeping it off with the dead girl still residing in her mind.

In the Jeep, Mike drove with a contemplative expression on his face. Raleigh stared out the window and thought perhaps he'd changed his mind and reconsidered any romantic notions towards her. The thought of dealing with this had to offer at least a slight pause.

"Do you think we know the girl?" Mike's voice startled her from her reverie.

Raleigh studied his face for any signs of bolting. Identity was always the difficult part. Since she inhabited the body, oftentimes she couldn't be certain of the person's identity. Even still, the most diffi-cult aspect came from the dying having to know what she could do in order to open the line of communication. Barbeaux Bayou gossip had spread the word of her abilities, but there always seemed to be a personal connection with murder.

Raleigh stared out the window. The fog had rolled in, making it difficult to see. "I keep hoping for someone we don't know."

Mike looked over. "We will find her through."

Raleigh's stomach lurched. An uneasy feeling told her that it wouldn't be simple this time.

THREE

The nibbles on her toes tickled. Her brain told her to pull away, to scratch, to make it stop, but her legs wouldn't listen to the command. Darkness ebbed around her as she floated in open space. A sharp pinch on her side pierced through the reverie, but she only felt lightness and an emptiness inside, no pain.

A loud bang rocked the tranquility of her floating form. She twitched, fighting the stupor of the water.

The pull of the water was heavy.

Sharp teeth sunk into her middle again. She felt a slight tickle this time.

A loud bang rolled through the water around her, and she flowed with the waves.

The realization vibrated in her head, and Raleigh lurched forward in her bed, gasping for air.

The rhythmic pounding continued from downstairs. She'd been dreaming of the dead girl.

She needed a shower.

The banging insisted on an answer at her front door. Raleigh glanced at the clock on her phone. 7:15. Girl Scouts must be working overtime to sell those cookies because anyone else would know not to show up at her house this early.

Slipping her jeans on under her nightgown, Raleigh took the stairs down two at a time. The third step from the bottom creaked as usual, and she nearly tripped over the laundry basket she'd left at the foot of the stairs. Even with the fogginess left behind by the dream, she could tell this wasn't going to be a great day.

Through the sunshine streaming in from the French door, the large looming figure of Sheriff Breaux stood banging, rattling the glass.

Swinging the door open, Raleigh caught him mid-rap, hoping to save her antique beveled glass from destruction. "Can I help you?"

He cleared his throat, hefting his portly belly up. "I'm here to take you in."

Raleigh leaned against the doorframe. "May I ask for what, or am I supposed to start trusting you after all our time together?"

He glared at her, unflinching. "Well, I reckon this morning a young girl was reported missing. Since you were so kind as to admit to knowing details of said disappearance, I figure that makes you my prime suspect."

Raleigh crossed her arms against her chest. "You know this won't end well for either of us, right?"

Sheriff Breaux raised a fist and then lowered it as he shook his head. "What I know, Ms. Cheramie is that I need to handle you myself since my deputies seem to have trouble with you. Now this doesn't make me happy, as you might imagine."

Raleigh turned away from him. "I'm going get dressed."

Sheriff Breaux stepped into the doorway. "I'm not going away, Ms. Cheramie."

Raleigh muttered to herself as she climbed back upstairs. "I wouldn't be so lucky."

After throwing on a comfortable sweatshirt, tossing some water in her face, and avoiding the mirrors, she climbed into the back of Sheriff Breaux's police cruiser. A huffy Breaux insisted she slide in like a common criminal. As she watched Jolie's house pass by, she wondered if Joey had identified the crawfish pond. Unlike her, Joey was a morning person. He'd probably already had two cups of coffee and tackled a mountain of paperwork. Before coming downstairs, she'd texted Mike to apprise him of the situation and to tell him that she'd be late for work this morning. This would put David and Mike in a bind, as on Fridays she wrote her Sunday stories. If the sheriff kept her as long as she thought he would, she'd be working most of her Saturday.

From the front seat, his thick jaw almost seemed to relax into a smile.

Raleigh scanned the parking lot as they pulled into the station. Full house today. "Who's the missing girl?"

It had to be the girl from the water. Barbeaux wasn't large enough for two women to go missing on the same night without it being advertised through all the gossip lines.

Sheriff Breaux pulled into his parking spot near the door labeled with a blue and white sign. "We'll get to that."

Raleigh allowed him to open the door, then she strolled into the station with her head up. Sheriff Breaux wouldn't turn her into that scared seventeen-year-old that he'd twisted until she didn't know what to say or how to react. She'd be thirty years old in April, and she would act like it for once.

The empty desks from last night were filled with sitting deputies, some on the telephone, some with propped up feet, and some slumped over mounds of paperwork. As the sheriff escorted her in, walking behind her as if he was bringing in an arrest, eyes turned to watch the procession. Some, like Nick, wouldn't meet Raleigh's eyes and returned to his paperwork.

Joey stepped away from a uniformed officer's desk and wrinkled his forehead as he puzzled over her. "What are you doing here this morning?"

"I'm bringing a suspect in for questioning," Sheriff Breaux said, jogging his head up and down as if he had music in his head.

"Why don't you bring us some coffee in interview room 2? Even that diesel fuel will be something when dealing with Ms. Cheramie."

Raleigh rolled her eyes at Joey and walked down the hall to the laminate wood door with a small placard above the frame labeling it Room 2. As a repeat visitor to the station, she didn't need directions to the interview rooms, so she'd at least keep some dignity and walk there on her own.

Inside the 8x8 room, Raleigh sank onto an eggshell blue chair and leaned back on two legs, waiting for Sheriff Breaux to close the door and pull out a chair that didn't seem capable of hefting his weight on its small pencil thin legs.

The two glared at each other from across the table. Nope. Raleigh didn't like him anymore now with the passage of eleven plus years.

He tapped a chubby index finger on top of a brown folder. "I've been waiting to have you in this room again for a long time."

Raleigh considered playing coy and getting under his skin, but then she thought about all the story prep she didn't have done yet for Sunday's paper.

"I'll save you some trouble," Raleigh said, setting her chair down and resting her hands on the table. "I was never alone last night. Mike and I left the Barbeaux Gazette at 5:30 and drove to Roxy's bar to meet Sheri. Donnie served us. At about 6:30, Madison called with a flat tire, and we went to meet her out by the canal bridge. At 8:00, we left her with a spare tire on her car and came here where we met Joey and Tyler."

Sheriff Breaux twisted at a black, plastic Timex watch that was worn white in spots. He glared at her, breathing noisy breaths. He should probably get that looked at, but Raleigh knew when to offer advice and when to keep quiet. Or at least she tried to know.

The door creaked open and Joey entered, holding two black mugs of coffee. He placed them down on the table, glancing over them. From his jacket pocket, he retrieved a miniature size Twix and placed it on the table in front of Raleigh.

The left side of his mouth curled up. The closest Joey came to a grin. "It's all I could find at the station."

Raleigh smiled up at him. Her family knew her so well. Sheriff Breaux glared at him, and he backed against the door, hanging his head.

Ripping open the packaging, she sunk her teeth into the chocolaty caramel goodness and felt her crankiness ebb. Even the sheriff's bulbous nose sniffing around her business across the table from her didn't seem unmanageable.

The sheriff sipped from the cup. "You understand I will verify this alibi of yours and find out if you are lying. Would you like to change anything to that statement now?"

Raleigh smiled. "That was my day. Nothing to change."

He twisted on his watch again. "So, in the course of your day, when did you learn about the missing young lady?"

Raleigh crossed her arms and leaned back in the chair again, knowing how this was going to go. "I discovered it while Mike and I were changing Madison's tire."

The sheriff narrowed his eyes. "Without any of your hocus pocus tales, how did you come to hear about it?"

"Well now, Me'Maw insists that I am a practicing Catholic." Raleigh smiled and raised her eyebrows. "So, no magic here, but the young lady made use of my Traiteur-to-the-dead connection and showed me some kind of crawfish pond."

Sheriff Breaux's fist banged down on the metal table three times. "Every time I deal with you, I want to bang my head against a wall. Now why is that? Are you working on that insanity defense?"

"Insanity pleas are only for the guilty."

Sheriff Breaux leaned back in his chair. "We both know there is blood on your hands."

Ross Blanch.

Raleigh scowled. The sheriff and many others would always bring it back to that one night when she'd defended herself, but no one would believe it back then, even with the physical evidence proving her story.

"Look," Raleigh said, uncrossing her legs and crossing them the other way. "Usually, I find the body, but this time I don't recognize the location. I've never been there before."

Joey cleared his throat. "She does have some specific details we're looking into that could offer us a lead."

Raleigh kept her eyes on Sheriff Breaux. A vein throbbed in his left temple, and his eyes darkened as he tried to remain quiet.

She leaned forward. "I know it's a crawfish pond because of the depth of the water and the cage. I also heard a boom like a cannon, and Pete said it could be sonic cannons. The noise caused a bunch of dogs to bark."

Raising his coffee mug, Sheriff Breaux drank deeply as his eyes glazed over in a faraway look.

He set his cup down on the table and pulled his shoulders up. "It sounds like you're talking about Ol' Leroy's place."

A thump echoed in Raleigh's head. Her unwanted visitor recognized the name, and excitement had risen.

"I just need to go out there, and I'm sure I'll be able to recognize the place."

The sheriff looked at Joey and frowned. "Ol' Leroy is a good family man; a hard worker. He'd never be involved in something sinister."

Joey nodded. "He may not know she's on the property. It's happened that way before."

The sheriff pounded the table again causing his mug to rattle. "We can't go searching on people's property on some hunch."

Raleigh leaned forward in the metal chair. "I will know that she's there. I will feel her."

The sheriff's lip curled in disgust. "Joey, take her out to Ol' Leroy's place and see if this is something other than hocus pocus while I check out her alibi." He glared at Raleigh one more time.

"You cannot search his property without a search warrant so don't try any funny business out there."

Joey motioned for Raleigh to follow him out. "We'll do it by the books, sir."

Bolting from the uncomfortable chair, Raleigh followed Joey out into the hall where people were talking and laughing. They stopped as the pair hurried through the station.

"I'd say we were lucky today," Joey whispered as they passed Detectives Max and Blanch speaking in hushed tones together near Max's office. "Let's hope we can continue to be lucky and find our girl."

Raleigh's stomach churned, the chocolate coating her esophagus and gut. This girl's luck had run out some time before the tire change and the connection last night. Now she clung to Raleigh like moss on an old cypress tree, waiting for resolution because it was all that Raleigh could offer.

FOUR

Raleigh felt the girl's anticipation curl around her legs and reach up her body like smoke as soon as she stepped out of Joey's squad car and onto the dirt road of Bitin' Tails Crawfish Farms. The unnamed, but familiar, girl lay somewhere among the reeds and the stagnant water, trembling with her desire to be found—all forecasted in Raleigh's brain as she tried to focus in on surveying for a location.

The road into the farm stretched and disappeared into a distant tree line. Crawfish ponds stretched to her right and her left, mere feet from the worn tracks of the path. A mud boat puttered to their right, headed in their direction. Its ruddy-faced driver shielded his eyes with a thick hand, peering at them as he steered with his free hand.

Joey fiddled with his cap on his head. "Anything?"

Raleigh inhaled the stench of stagnant water and dead crawfish, attempting to settle her nerves to get a clearer signal as to the young lady's exact whereabouts. "She's here."

Feeling a faint tug to the right, Raleigh picked her way through the overgrown weeds, following the beacon.

At a patch of grass right off the levee embankment, she stopped. Murky water greeted her, littered with blades of old stalks of rice.

The boat slid onto land to her left as she peered intently, trying to distinguish some form in the muddy water and grass.

A gentleman, whose face was toughened by the sun, stepped out of the boat. "Can I help you, Officer?"

Reaching up, he removed his hat from his bald head and wiped the sweat with a gray rag from his back pocket. Raleigh would place him in the 50s-60s range from his wiry eyebrows, but she knew that the outside work could have weathered him and turned his face to the deep bronze that peered expectantly at them now.

Joey tipped his own cap in his direction. "We had a tip that the body of a missing girl may have been disposed of last night in one of your ponds."

Raleigh squinted against the glare of the sunlight, trying to focus on the conversation, but the girl's voice in her head had become more frantic.

The man scanned the wide expanse. "That's impossible. The property is locked tight every night. No one can get in."

"We drove right in this morning." Joey kicked at the dirt. "The lock wasn't snapped shut."

"Well, dammit, my son would forget to come home if he wasn't hungry." Leroy gritted his teeth, shaking his head. "But no one would know he'd forgotten to lock it up yesterday after I told him to let the dogs loose before he left. I just don't see how a body could be back here." He glanced around again, rubbing a hand over his head. "You said a young woman?"

Raleigh waved her hand over her targeted area. "I believe she may be in this vicinity."

Leroy squinted at her through brown eyes the color of tree bark. "Do I know you? You look familiar."

Raleigh put her hand out for him to shake. He hesitated, but then rubbed his hand against his stained jeans and gripped hers firmly. "I don't think we've met before, but I'd really appreciate it if you check out this spot. I'm sure you'd want to know if there was a young woman here."

Leroy shook his head, still puzzling over her face. "Let me get my rake. I'll prove to you that this is impossible. I mean how would you know it's right there anyways." Leroy turned towards his boat and muttered, "She looks so familiar. Can't place her."

Raleigh missed the rest of his muttering as he walked to the boat and returned with what appeared to be more of a hook tool that must be used to catch the crawfish traps and pull them into the boat. Gripping it in one hand, Leroy approached the edge of the water and peered into the surface. Eyeing the tool, Raleigh wished Leroy would turn it over to her, but from his firm grip, she could see his desire to be in charge.

Dipping it in near the edge, he poked around some, but didn't venture wide. Raleigh waited for him to expand the search, but he continued prodding the same spot. Growing anxious, she pointed toward the grassy area and held her hand out until he relented. With a frown crinkling his forehead, he reached out and pushed his hook at a superficial level. His tool jerked forward then backward as something snagged, ending his haphazard prodding.

Pulling upwards, an elbow broke the surface followed by an opalescent hand. He gasped and lunged backward, the hook releasing its catch. "Summa bitch."

He dropped his pole on the bank, his hands shaking. "We need to get her outta there. I can't have her in my pond."

"We will," Raleigh assured him, turning to Joey, who'd lifted his phone to his ear as he stepped away. "Joey will have someone here soon, and they will take her out."

He tugged at an ear, and his eyes twitched as he stepped aimlessly in a semicircle. "This could ruin me! Not that I'm not sorry about the girl, understand? But I've worked so hard for this business every damn day. I fight the damn birds, the crazy luck of the weather, and the barometric pressure, not to mention the cutthroat market wanting to undersell me. *Now* I have to deal with someone dumping a body into my pond? This will end me."

Ol' Leroy's eyes watered, and he wrung his hands on his loose pants. The dead body had been too much for him. Shock, maybe?

"Do you have any family I can call?" Raleigh asked, thinking about how she liked her Paw around when she felt the world falling apart.

He shook his head. "I'll be alright. If my old lady sees this, she'll have nightmares for months. She'd have us moved and all that humdrum."

The people Raleigh met weren't experiencing their best day. She knew on a better day, Barbeaux Bayou had empathetic people. They certainly didn't lack charisma.

Fifteen minutes later the area swarmed with the people needed to process a crime scene and recover the body. The local coroner was also the local emergency doctor, and the dive team that recovered water submerges also ran line with local oil pipelines. All these side hustles were required to keep this small town running smoothly. Even the local press/ construction worker showed up when Mike's Jeep pulled in behind Joey's cruiser.

"Did I miss anything?" Mike slipped his recorder in his pocket as he lumbered over behind the yellow crime scene tape where Raleigh had been relegated. At least Joey appeared remorseful, but he walked a very tight line with her, and she didn't wish to cause him any more trouble.

Raleigh grimaced as she rubbed the deep indentation of the scar on her wrist for comfort. "They are about to bring her up."

Forcing herself to look back in the direction of Buddy, the diver who'd been only a few years ahead of them in high school, she watched as they fumbled with gears and metal ropes, attempting to offer a wide girth to the body so as not to disturb the evidence any further than necessary. A makeshift gurney had been secured under her body, and from Buddy's thumbs up to his father in the driver seat of the lift truck, Raleigh assumed she was ready to be brought to the surface.

No matter how many times she saw a dead body, she had never

been prepared for the sight. Each time she'd felt like bolting or hiding behind the nearest person for strength.

Squeaking and churning proceeded, and water cascaded around the legs of the three men in the water. As matted hair and translucent flesh emerged from the ruddy water, Raleigh swallowed and forced herself to look.

Even with the swollen face and bloated body, Raleigh recognized Emma. The same Emma she hadn't followed yesterday at Roxy's bar

She gasped. "Mike."

Pain crawled through her throat, but the space in her head lay empty. She'd left with the assurance that her body had been found.

But what had happened to her?

Mike's arms wrapped around her from behind, his warmth touching the chill that had crawled in and taken hold. He leaned down to close in the distance of their height. "I know what you're thinking, and it's not your fault."

Raleigh shook her head. Her throat felt as if it had collapsed. She scratched out. "We should have gone after her."

Mike squeezed tighter. She could feel his heat piercing the iciness of her internal thoughts. "As a teenager, she wasn't listening to us. She barely knew us."

"She was only sixteen. We could have..." Raleigh trailed off, unsure what they could have done. Neither of them knew Emma's parents. A few weeks ago, they'd been asked to help guide the journalism class in reinstituting their school newspaper after a decade, and David had insisted as part of a community outreach program. They'd shown up for a few classes since, and they didn't even know the student's last names yet. As usual, logical Mike was right. These kids didn't trust them, and with everything in their worlds, Raleigh didn't blame them.

Max's navy-blue Caprice entered the fray of cars, and Raleigh watched him walk towards Joey, who now stood with the coroner, speaking in hushed tones.

As a lead detective, the case would probably be assigned to Max even though Joey had pursued it. Sheriff Breaux had strict levels of hierarchy, not to mention Joey carried the Cheramie moniker. The name meant Joey would be forced to fight the bias of Sheriff Breaux his entire career—or at least until the man was no longer sheriff.

As Max approached Joey, his eyes lingered over the mud boat, the reeds, and a haphazard crab trap that had been tossed during the search. Raleigh tried to follow his study of the scene, his typical sweep, but from their distance, she couldn't see the details.

Max reached Joey and Joey shook his head. With a grimace and a jerk of his arm, Joey expressed his frustration.

Raleigh watched their lips move, but the words didn't travel the one hundred feet. Then Joey's voice rose, carrying above the ruckus of the scene.

"You need to get your head on the case. Put the victims first and get past this vendetta you have."

Max growled. "It's none of your business how I handle my case."

Joey pointed toward the milling people on the scene. "That girl's parents are going to have to identify her in that condition. We could have found her last night if you would have spoken up."

Max scanned the area and he and Raleigh's eyes met. His furrowed brow and grimace spoke of anger. "What are you saying?"

Joey shook his head. "Do your job. Do what's right." He then walked off toward Ol' Leroy, who sat on the back bed of a pick-up truck a distance away from the scene.

Max scowled in Raleigh's direction one last time before moving in to talk to Buddy, who'd surfaced with something Raleigh couldn't see from her vantage point. The object fit in the palm of his hand and didn't allow for a peek.

Max motioned for an officer, who brought over a manila envelope and the object disappeared inside.

Joey approached Raleigh with his cap in his hand. "Sheriff says I'm to take you in for a written and signed statement."

Raleigh squinted at him, smiling. "I bet he said confession."

Joey placed his hands on his hips. "Well, the man does tend to chew on a dead point. Soon, we'll have a suspect, and you'll be alright."

"Need me to come with you?" Mike asked. "Be your alibi?"

"No, you stay and get the story," Raleigh said, following Joey. "Who knows what evidence I may need to keep me from life in prison."

Mike chuckled as he stretched his tall, lanky form. "Don't give him too hard of a time or at least not harder than he deserves."

Raleigh laughed, but then cut herself short. A teenager had died. It wasn't the time to laugh.

FIVE

Mike held up a mock-up sheet. "The notes say the ad was a half-pager."

Raleigh squinted at the message scribbled on a sticky note stuck to a full-page political ad. Her eyes watered under the stress of four hours at the computer screen in an attempt to fit everything onto the twelve pages they'd sold ad space for this week. After a brief mention of yesterday's horrendous findings in Bitin' Tails Crawfish Ponds, Raleigh had been able to trim a parish council story decision on building permits, which had helped out with the hours of work she'd missed yesterday. Mike had covered her story on the break-in at the old lumberyard, so she'd managed to catch up, somewhat.

But then Rachel had taken vacation and left her notes as a replacement, except neither of them was having success deciphering them.

Stringing the letters together, Raleigh guessed at the meaning. "The message says 'I attached the full-page ad file as you've requested. As per our arrangement, this ad will run each Sunday for the next six weeks.'"

Mike finger combed his hair, his jaw set with his frustration. "Why do they always oversell when Rachel is on vacation?"

Raleigh shrugged, tossing the notes onto the desk. "We don't care if they oversell when she's not on vacation because we don't have to fix it."

The Barbeaux Gazette shared advertising sales with the television station. Since the money existed in television, Rachel devoted her time to that medium. The television, and even the radio station, appeared to do well now, but advertising didn't appear concerned about print space. With the trouble with newspaper in the current climate, Raleigh assumed this was just a sign of the times.

Mike looked over the mock-up pages again. "What about shrinking it this week and offering a deal?"

Raleigh stared at the ad on the screen—a smiling sheriff stared back. "We could suggest starting the run next week—or never."

Mike made a mark on page 4 with a pencil. "I'm all for that solution, but David would have our jobs."

"And then where would he find two reporters who would work for the pennies he pays us?"

"True," Mike said. "So, what do we do about the sheriff's ad?"

"A half page this week, and offer him an extra week to make up for it?" Raleigh said. "We have a few months before the election, so he'll likely be buying more. And if we are lucky, someone will be running against him, and we can put their advertisements side by side."

Mike sank back into his chair, the wheels squirming under the added weight. "You think someone will run against him?"

Raleigh made a few clicks and shrunk the size of the advertisement, so it would be ready to insert into the layout. "I think we should recruit someone to run against him."

Mike's lip curved upward in a smirk. "Like who?"

Raleigh shrugged. "I don't know. Have any ideas? It can't be Max because he sure won't help us."

"Maybe Joey? He's the do-right type, and definitely would be an in for us on all the cases."

Raleigh twirled in her chair as she considered it. The imbalance of equilibrium always jumpstarted the creative juices. "Think the family connection would be a hindrance?"

Mike swiped a stress ball from his desk and tossed it in the air. "People love Me'Maw and Paw. You aren't so bad yourself now that you've stuck around and didn't let them forget the real you."

Raleigh spun around again. Joey could be an interesting option. He'd rally the average Joe of Barbeaux but not the elite, but the common people outnumbered the wealthy anyway.

A rapping on the front desk sounded through the open window into the workroom. "Hello?"

Raleigh and Mike exchanged a look. No one came in on Saturday unless they were working, and then they had to have an ID card to scan into the building. The only way someone could have entered the building was if Mrs. Betty Marjorie was really losing it and had left the front door open on Friday afternoon.

Mike walked out of the cubicle and toward the front desk. Raleigh stared at the sticky notes she'd stuck in haphazard fashion all over her cubicle wall. She'd been gathering sources and intel to write an in-depth piece about a recent local drug epidemic. Sources and the notes appeared to have vomited all over her workspace, but she still didn't have an angle on the story.

Lathan Babin trailed behind Mike toward the cubicle area. Dressed casually in jeans, a gray V-neck T-shirt, and loafers he appeared younger than his thirty-two years. After spending only a few weeks volunteering in the journalism class, Raleigh knew that Lathan enjoyed the spoils of being an attractive young, single teacher. He could sweet-talk the sweet old lady cafeteria workers and the hardline history teacher as well. With the students, he made an effort to be cool and stay abreast with the hip gossip. His students liked it as much as his principal.

Raleigh spun to face him. "Coming to check on the project?"

"No, no, no," Lathan said, sinking into one of the rolling chairs at a nearby empty cubicle. "I got a call this morning from the school about Emma. I thought you two might be able to tell me more because I don't know how I'm supposed to handle my students on Monday. I don't understand how this could happen."

Mike's chair squeaked as he sat down. "We don't know many details yet. She was found out in a crawfish pond. We're waiting to see if it's drowning or something happened before she went into the water. Either way, it will likely be ruled as a homicide."

Raleigh looked at his downcast look. He appeared concerned about his student. "Did you hear any talk about something going on with her?"

Lathan's head picked up and glanced around the office "Teenagers talk. They don't know how to keep anything to themselves. It's typically just idle gossip."

"But?" Raleigh prompted, feeling as if there was something he should be saying. Something more.

He shrugged, blowing air through his lips. "Just last week there was some trouble at home, and she spent the night in her car. All I heard was that her father wouldn't let her in the house. I reported it to guidance after hearing her discussing it in class. Protocol and all, but I didn't overhear the details as she kept it particularly hushed."

Mike jotted words down on a sticky note that was near him. "That brings the parents under question."

"I don't think she has..." Lathan grimaced, "...had a good home life. According to the class gossip, the boyfriend adds to the issues with the parents."

Raleigh remembered Jeremy's hand twisting Emma's forearm and questioned herself yet again for letting her go. "We had a glimpse of the boyfriend issue Thursday at Roxy's. I'd say he's definitely under question."

"He's an interesting fellow," Lathan said, shaking his head. "I've been meaning to join y'all Thursday happy hour crew, but I always end up volunteering for something after school."

Mike tapped his pen against a notepad. "A group of journalism students were at Roxy's Thursday night."

Lathan's eyebrows rose. "At a bar?"

"Yep," Raleigh said. "They left when we tried to ask them that very same question. Did they mention it in class Friday?"

He shook his head. "They were real quiet and didn't really want to talk or work. I knew something was wrong, so I chalked it up to Emma being missing. They've been arguing lately over petty things. Who gets what story, who did a better job, who should have the morning announcements, and everything really."

Mike scribbled on his sticky note again while Raleigh's mind dwelled on what possible trouble teenagers would have today. Eleven years ago, she and Mike had found themselves in a mess as seniors in high school, so she knew that the means could have no bounds. Discovering what had happened to Emma may mean untangling whatever they were hiding.

Lathan stood, smoothing out the nonexistent wrinkle in his shirt. "I need to get going. I'm going to be helping with the music at The Seafood Shack tonight. Raleigh, if you aren't busy, you should come check it out."

Raleigh's face heated as his pointed invitation fell in the room. Mike buried himself with his notes and avoided looking their way, which for some reason made it more awkward. Lathan had not included him so it couldn't be misunderstood what he meant. At least she didn't think she'd misunderstood.

Raleigh struggled to find the words to respond, knowing she would not be showing up. "I'll see what time we get out of here."

He nodded as his eyes slid over her, and he headed toward the lobby doors.

The silence in the office grew as Mike busied himself with a notepad, reading silently through some notes. Lathan had enough time to reach the high school before Raleigh couldn't handle the growing tension in the room.

Raleigh leaned back in her chair, so that she could see Mike's full facial reaction, even though his face studied the notes intently. "That was weird, right?"

Mike remained staring at his notes, pencil poised to write further. "As a teacher, I'm sure he's concerned for his students."

Raleigh wanted to shake him. "I meant him mentioning tonight and not inviting both of us."

Mike looked up and grinned. "C'mon, the guy was trying to ask you out."

Raleigh frowned. "But I'm not his type. I'm like eight years older than the women he dates. Have you listened to any of the gossip? He likes them barely legal to drink."

Mike's forehead furrowed. "True, but men eventually figure out that they need someone they can hold a conversation with."

Raleigh laughed. "Are you sure? I think most men would disagree. They have probably wished I would talk less."

Mike chuckled, revealing his dimple. "Like I said, it takes us longer to grow up and figure out what's important."

He hadn't told her not to go out with Lathan though. Was she supposed to date while they were waiting this proper time for her to get over Max? Was he dating? This whole relationship business was confusing. And she certainly didn't want to risk a lifetime friendship on uncertainty.

Raleigh yanked her notes from under the pile of sticky notes David had left them for the day's paper. According to the agreement with his wife, their editor took off two Saturdays a month to spend with his wife anyway she wished. She held him to it just like their marriage counselor had told her to do, so he never came in even for days like this. Lucky him. Even her boss's relationship affected her life. Everywhere she looked, she was confronted by a faucet of life shaped by relationships. She and Mike needed to get this paper done, so she could get out of here.

SIX

"Hand me that spoon, dear." Gripping the lid of the Magnalite pot, Me'Maw peered into her pot roast while she waved her free hand at Raleigh.

Raleigh turned toward the counter and puzzled over the four stainless steel spoons laid out waiting their turn to stir in their pots. She picked up the one that appeared to have residue of the light brown pot gravy and handed it over to Me'Maw's waiting hand.

Raleigh asked, "Are you sure I can't help?"

Me'Maw glanced away from her pots with a smile. "Why don't you get the plates and utensils ready?"

Madison swung through the door. "Mom says to get another tablecloth?"

"The hall closet," Raleigh said, pulling plates out of the cabinet.

Squeaking along the linoleum floor, Mason ran in through the back door and swung around his mama's hips just as Annabeth, Joey's youngest, dashed in red-faced after him.

Madison threw her arms up as his impact turned her a few steps. "Mason John, we run outside, especially with all these people here today."

"Sorry, Mommy," he called as he escaped down the hall, Annabeth on his heels, her braids flapping behind her as she giggled. Raleigh watched, plates in hands, feeling as if she'd been taken back in time to Sunday dinners with her and Joey running around in the same manner.

"Ah," Me'Maw said, looking back at Raleigh, knowing. "I remember like it was yesterday when it was you two running in the house."

Madison groaned. "I've become my mother."

Madison had thought Me'Maw meant the two of them, but Me'Maw had always had a way to see inside Raleigh's thoughts.

"It could be worse," Uncle Jude said, stomping through the back door, getting the mud from his boots all over the rug.

Madison raised her eyebrows. "How?"

He chuckled. "I don't know, but it could."

Madison shook her head before turning to walk down the hall to retrieve the tablecloth.

Uncle Jude had a weird sense of humor. He tended to make jokes that no one else found the humor in. Perhaps Joey's serious nature had come at the hand of being embarrassed growing up by his father's corniness. Or maybe he'd been born that way. They'd never know.

The screen door snapped again as Mike entered. "Paw and I have the ice chest of canned drinks on the back porch."

Me'Maw rattled the spoon against the metal pot and then shut the burner off. "I believe Sunday dinner is ready."

The screen door creaked open again. She should find something to prop it open with all the traffic before the spring popped. "Then, I'm just in time with the bread." Raleigh's mom entered carrying a large wheat germ colored basket. "The first batch came out too dark, so I had to try again."

"Oh, nonsense," Mike said, taking the basket from her. "I could have used it as a bowl for Me'Maw's roast."

Raleigh's mom chuckled, her hazel eyes crinkling at the corners in webs. "Raleigh, you're going to need to learn how to cook to keep him happy."

Raleigh opened her mouth to object—she knew how to cook, she just didn't cook—but Paw walked in through the back door. "Me'Maw will take care of that boy like she's done since he's been knee high." Paw motioned his hand a little above his knee and winked at Raleigh. "Raleigh Lynn just needs to hang on to him."

Mike smirked, but he didn't correct him. He left that up to her. Raleigh jutted her chin out and raised her eyebrows. Breaking Paw's heart was not on the menu for this Sunday family dinner.

"Let's get those children fed." Me'Maw peered at Raleigh, seeing right through her as if she were an opaque window. Not for the first time, Raleigh wished it would work in reverse. Perhaps Me'Maw could tell her what to do about Mike.

She didn't get a chance to bring it up as the kitchen filled to its bursting point as Cheramies descended and clattered dishes and called for more bread as they served themselves Sunday dinner, a tradition that had once been in place every Sunday when Raleigh was growing up. That was before everyone became too busy to show up. Raleigh had disappeared long before that when she'd moved away, but Me'Maw had requested that this Sunday everyone come, and everyone was here, even cousin Jolie, Joey's sister. The thirty-five-year-old nurse who never associated with the family was now perched on a chair with Me'Maw's good China balanced precariously in her lap as she fought with her toddler to take a bite, who'd prefer running around the kitchen, offering everyone a slobbery kiss.

The Cheramie women, some born Cheramies like Jolie and others married into like her mother, crowded around the laminate table, discussing recipes that had been passed down to them through mothers and mothers-in-laws. All of these women could cook and had claims to a special recipe. Raleigh had eaten their dishes a time or two at family gatherings and could say that they were good at gumbos and sauces, not to mention blackberry tarts (Aunt Linda). Getting them all in one place meant an opportunity for them to lay claims to their greatness and share these self-celebrated dishes with each other.

Raleigh had nothing to share with these women. In fact, if she mentioned the prepackaged dinners and the take-out she subsisted on, they'd gasp and insist on cooking lessons. If she hadn't learned it at the elbow of Me'Maw since she was two feet tall, she would never learn it. It was the putting it to use that presented a struggle.

The men had escaped with heaping plates out to the front porch. She would bet the topic of conversation wasn't the secret ingredient in the dirty rice. The women didn't even glance her way when she escaped the kitchen, hoping for better luck among the Cheramie men.

In the living room, the plates of food lay abandoned on the children's table as they peered at the screen blaring out the dramatic overture of a cartoon.

Mason glanced up as Raleigh passed through, his eyes big in his 'I want something' way. "Nanan, can we go outside and play now?"

Raleigh leaned in and whispered, "Mom said you had to eat all your lunch first, and I'm not getting in trouble with her, but make it disappear and neither of us are in trouble."

A giggle escaped as he squirmed in his seat. "Gotcha, Nanan."

Raleigh winked and continued out the front door. She'd probably be in trouble for that later because what five-year-old kept a secret? But she'd still be the cool Nanan. She could live with that. On the wide front porch, Paw sat back in his well-worn rocking chair, an empty plate near his foot and a toothpick dangling from his lip. He chewed on that wooden stick as he listened to his sons and grandsons talk about the price of crawfish and shrimp. Uncle Jude made his livelihood on the deck of a shrimping boat, and the rest of the year he farmed his land and tinkered with a tractor like Paw. Sitting next to him in his favorite antique rocking chair on the porch was Raleigh's dad, who worked in the heat of a shipyard all day where he advertised his brother's latest haul, occasionally helping him out when he was short a deckhand. His gardening expertise extended to helping his dad with his if only absolutely necessary. He'd had enough of tending the land growing up, and over the back-breaking work of the garden, he'd prefer to buy his vegetables if it came to it much to his dad's chagrin.

Sitting on the worn wooden planks of the porch, Uncle Camille leaned against a post, gazing off in the direction of Raleigh's parents' home, his eyes unfocused. His skin tone appeared yellowish and his frame skeletal. Once the man had done odd jobs. He'd worked with both brothers a time or two; he'd even gardened when his daughter was in elementary school. Now he wasted away.

Jolie's husband, Will, sat quietly next to Joey and discussed shrimping with the others, although Raleigh couldn't imagine how he'd ever had time for it. Will was a local pharmacist, and he wasn't nearly as uptight as Jolie, but with uncalloused hands and alabaster skin that didn't look as though it had ever been kissed by the sun, Raleigh couldn't imagine he'd spend much time in the heat on a trawl boat. Mike sat off at the end of the porch, spread out with multiple plates of food. He interjected comments into the conversation having the knowledge of all the stories he'd written for the Barbeaux Gazette. She'd never known him to shrimp or crawfish before, and she certainly didn't count them chasing those crawfish holes in the ditch as children.

Paw tapped the arm of his rocker. "Have a seat, Raleigh Lynn. I imagine the conversation inside couldn't hold your attention."

Raleigh smiled and then sank into an empty chair next to him. She'd probably spent more time with these men than she'd ever had with the women in the house, discounting Me'Maw.

Uncle Jude put an empty plate down next to his chair and turned to Raleigh. "How's it living in the old house?"

"Great," Raleigh said, rocking forward in her chair. "Aunt Clarice had so much stuff that I still haven't unpacked all the boxes yet."

Uncle Jude laughed. "She sure did like her travels. I remember when I was younger visiting her just to see what outrageous item she'd brought back on her latest trip."

Raleigh's dad nodded. "As I remember she had a few things from Grand'Mere, too. You may want to keep an eye out for those. They should be valuable antiques."

Joey broke off a piece of bread and squinted as if he were considering every atom of the slice. "I remember this plastic sleeve of Confederate money she used to have in that glass armoire. I used to look at that every time I visited."

Raleigh nodded, thinking back to her own childhood when she'd spent time studying Aunt Clarice's collections. There'd always been something new to discover like jade hair combs or a healing crystal she'd had blessed from some shaman. "I remember that. It must still be in one of those boxes in the spare room that I haven't unpacked. I haven't seen any of those items from the armoire yet."

Mike winked. "If you'd clean that room out, you could get a roommate and help pay that house note." They'd discussed this a few times, but Raleigh procrastinated going through Aunt Clarice's remaining items, especially when the woman's ghost could pop up during the sorting. The woman was known to decorate as she saw fit, leaving Raleigh feeling as though she were losing her mind.

A motion from the driveway caught her peripheral vision, and she turned to watch a male figure step out from behind Uncle Jude's navy blue pick-up truck.

Mike followed her gaze. "Jeremy, what are you doing here?"

"I needed to talk to Ms. C." Jeremy twitched and his eyes darted from one face to another on the porch. His dark hair appeared disheveled, but his face looked exhausted.

Raleigh stood, meeting Mike's leveled gaze for a moment before returning to Jeremy. "Sure."

Raleigh walked down the porch steps, passed Uncle Camille who didn't blink as she interrupted his line of sight and crossed over into the side yard, watching Jeremy twitch with his hands in the pockets of his cargo pants. As she approached, he made a few steps further as he watched the gentleman study them from the porch, but Raleigh set both feet firmly on the ground and stood, waiting.

"What's going on?" Raleigh asked.

He stopped mid-step and turned to face her while releasing a huff of air forcefully through his nose. "Isn't that the question? I know you are the one who found Emma. Everyone in town's talking about it."

"None of the talk matters." Raleigh noticed his jittery arm movements and his eyes not losing sight of the worn grass. "What matters is finding out the truth about what happened to her."

He laughed harshly. "The truth. I know what you think is the truth. What you think about me. Well, I didn't do anything to her."

Raleigh remained calm, though his face had reddened and his voice had risen. Clearly, Jeremy had a temper. "No one said you did, Jeremy."

Jeremy flung his hands in the air. "You may as well have said it. Everyone's talking about how you dissed me that night, thought I was going to hurt her. Now the police want to talk to me. No one will believe me now because of you."

Raleigh stood her ground, unflinching as he began pacing in a jerking manner. "What did happen that night?"

"You think I know?" he shouted. "I just need you to tell everyone that I didn't do anything to her, so that they will leave me alone."

Raleigh felt a brush against the small of her back and glanced up to see Mike step in beside her.

"What's the problem, Jeremy?" Mike asked.

Jeremy's eyes darkened into discs. "Make her tell everyone that I didn't hurt Emma. Stop playing cool with the kids and messin' with my life. Y'all know nothin' about what's going on, but y'all accuse a man. Is it because I'm Mexican? No one will stand up for me anyway, right?"

Raleigh felt the palpable tension growing around Jeremy as his anger reached dangerous proportions. "Then, tell us what happened so we can help you."

Jeremy shrugged his shoulders and threw his hands up in the air. "This was a waste of my time—I can't trust anyone."

He turned and stalked off. Raleigh stepped forward to stop him, thinking about how she'd let Emma go Thursday night, but Mike's hand clamped down on her shoulder gently holding her back.

At the end of the driveway, he jumped into a beat up, rust colored Ford Ranger and drove off, tires squealing.

It didn't sit well in Raleigh's gut. They shouldn't have let him go.

Mike shook his head as she looked at him. "He'll need to calm down some before he tells us anything."

Raleigh sighed. She hoped nothing happened to him before that time.

Joey lumbered over, gazing off in the direction Jeremy's truck had disappeared. "So, I hear he's gotten word that we're looking for him. Word travels fast through Barbeaux—the gossip and the truth."

Rubbing the smooth indentation of the scar on her wrist, Raleigh considered Jeremy's words and agitated behavior. "It won't make him look innocent if he avoids talking to the police."

"Nope," Joey said, raising his hands to his hips. "But something must be going on. What do you two know about the boy?"

"Not much." Mike shrugged. "He didn't actually belong in the journalism class, but he did hang out often. Lathan didn't seem to mind."

"He and Emma were always a pair," Raleigh added. "He'd help out with hauling papers, carrying equipment, and all because he wanted to be with Emma."

Mike nodded. "He didn't let Emma do much without him."

"I see." Joey chewed on his bottom lip. "Odds are he didn't let her run off by herself Thursday."

Raleigh shuddered. Maybe that had been an elaborate act.

Mike grimaced. "They weren't alone when they left Roxy's though. There was a group of them."

Joey's head bobbed downward. "Yep, and none of them want to say much. They all look guilty at this point, but Jeremy is the only one evading our inquiry."

Raleigh thought about what Jeremy had said. Was it fear causing him to avoid the police? She didn't know enough about the boy to say. She didn't want to judge before she knew the facts. That's what had happened to her in high school, and she couldn't put another teenager through that experience.

She needed to find out more about this group of kids. Emma deserved to have the truth be known. Raleigh's responsibility was always to the dead.

SEVEN

Waiting for a response to her knock, Raleigh took in the peeling paint, the rotten porch boards, and the broken rocker leaning against the cracked siding. An older model sedan sat surrounded by aluminum cans, boxes of rusted metal junk, and bulging trash bags. Raleigh banged on the door louder, hearing a blaring television inside.

Dragging feet vibrated through the floorboards. She and Mike exchanged looks and waited.

When the door creaked open, a hefty woman glared at them from a 45-degree crack in the door. Looking from Mike to Raleigh, her hand seemed poised to shut it in their faces, even though they'd called before their arrival.

She exhaled, her entire body shifting with the effort before opening the door wider and stepping through it. "My husband's sleeping after working the night shift, so I'll talk outside."

Mike and Raleigh stepped back, allowing her ample room to hobble out and move toward the green plastic lawn chairs scattered around the front porch.

Raleigh cleared her throat. "We are so sorry for your loss, Mrs. Rogers."

She frowned, the mole near her lip dipping with her upper lip. "It's Mrs. Cohn. Emma's dad was killed in a car accident when she was one. Keith here is her stepfather. He treated her decent though."

The door creaked opened again. "Mom, I'm going to Lindsey's house."

Mrs. Cohn motioned with a sun-spotted hand. "Dani, these people are here asking about your sister."

Dani had the same deep chestnut hair as Emma, even the same tiny nose. Their eyes differed slightly. Dani's had more of an almond shape and her cheekbones were more pronounced.

Mike stepped toward her and extended his hand for her to shake. "Do you have a minute to tell me something about your sister?"

Dani's eyes slid toward her mother, but then back to Mike. "Sure."

Mike's buff, blond surfer-meets-nerd look tended to attract the young and old alike. He hadn't stayed single this long from lack of options.

Engaging Dani in a talk about the Foreigner T-shirt she wore, Mike led her off the porch toward the faded maroon car. From Raleigh's spot on the porch, she and Mike were in eyesight, and she knew he'd maneuvered it that way.

Raleigh turned her attention to the mother.

"Did Emma have any trouble recently that you could tell me about?"

Mrs. Cohn guffawed. "Emma came with nothing but trouble. Always something with that girl."

Raleigh prompted, "Such as?" From the few weeks in class, Emma had been the quiet girl who'd volunteered to answer all their questions. Raleigh had classified her as an intellectual, a college-bound girl.

Mrs. Cohn wiped her forehead with a rag clutched in her hands. "She was needy. Always needed me to be at school for a parent meeting. And don't get me started on those other parents—her so called friends who always thought they were better than us with their fancy parties and dress codes. She'd beg Keith for expensive clothes that we couldn't afford. The man works fifty hours a week in a shipyard, and it wasn't to buy Ms. Priss a fancy dress."

Mrs. Cohn sat in silence for a moment and then dabbed at a few tears at the corner of her eyes. Those were harsh words, though, from someone who'd lost her daughter only days ago, but perhaps she'd coated her grief in anger.

Raleigh pushed ahead. "Did she ever have problems with any of the students at school?"

Mrs. Cohn shook her head. "She wasn't bullied if that's what you're askin'. Everyone liked her as far as I could tell. She spent more time with those friends of hers than her family for sure. Didn't really think we were good enough, I guess."

A deep animalistic groan rumbled in her chest and escaped from her trembling lips.

Raleigh waited until she settled again, when the dabs at her eyes dwindled. "Is that what you fought about that caused her to sleep in her car?" Raleigh patted Mrs. Cohn on her knee, hoping to show some sympathy, although the woman hadn't shown much remorse for her daughter's death yet with her biting words.

Thick hands clutched her chest, yanking away from Raleigh. "How do you know about that?"

Raleigh offered her most sympathetic expression, hoping to inspire the idea that she was on the mother's side. "A friend of hers offered that information."

Mrs. Cohn frowned. "She'd lied to Keith about where she'd been for the weekend. She was supposed to sleep at Olivia's or Sara's, I can't remember now, but then she showed up in the middle of the night and said she couldn't sleep over and she wouldn't tell us why. Then, Olivia comes over and says she hadn't seen Emma at all over the weekend, but Emma wouldn't tell Keith what's going on."

"So, she slept in the car?"

"She was stubborn like her daddy." Mrs. Cohn shook her head. "Keith told her to sleep outside until she told him the truth. He didn't think she'd actually do it."

Raleigh nodded, considering what she knew about Emma. None of this meshed with the girl from the classroom. "So maybe she was just as stubborn Thursday night."

Fiddling with her rag, Mrs. Cohn huffed. "She missed curfew and didn't pick up Dani at the basketball game. Dani hitched a ride from a neighbor and didn't tell us until the morning. She thought she was covering for her sister."

Mrs. Cohn looked off in the direction of Mike and Dani. Raleigh followed and noticed that Mike had Dani laughing through a tear-streaked face. She had his full attention—or so it seemed, and she blushed with it.

"You shouldn't be here."

Raleigh turned to the other side of the porch where the voice had come from and saw Jeremy standing with his arms crossed, glaring at the two of them.

Raleigh exhaled, nervous for Mrs. Cohn with Jeremy's uncontrollable temper. "We were just talking about Emma. Would you like to join us?"

Jeremy waved his arm in their direction, his lip curling as if he was going to spit at them. "I can imagine what you are saying."

Standing, Raleigh stepped toward him, wondering if she should ease him away from Mrs. Cohn. "We want to figure out what happened to Emma. I'm sure you want to know that as well."

"Of course, I do," Jeremy spit out, eliminating a few steps between the porch and them. "I just don't want people blaming it on me."

"You need to leave young man." Mrs. Cohn coughed with the force of her words but rattled on. "I've told you before that you aren't welcome here."

Jeremy laughed harshly, sneering at Mrs. Cohn. "Emma wasn't

really welcomed here either, right? But I'm sure you'll play the part of the sad Mama and get the attention you wanted."

Mrs. Cohn heaved herself out of the chair, clenching her gown near her chest with both fists. "Get off my property, and do not come back here."

"Jeremy, we need to talk." Raleigh leapt off the porch, feeling the jarring force of the impact send waves up her legs and hips as her boots landed. A move like that should probably only be done after exercise.

Jeremy shook his head. "I have nothing for you. I'm going to find out what happened myself." Jeremy hurried off to his truck with its engine still running in the next-door neighbor's driveway.

As Jeremy drove away, Mike and Dani joined her in front of the porch.

Jeremy behaved as if were guilty—lurking around, refusing to speak to the police—but he spoke as if he didn't know what had happened. Around school, he was known as the quiet boy who didn't participate in any school activities, but he followed Emma around to all of hers.

Mrs. Cohn sank back into her chair. "He's not welcome here."

Mike leaned against the front porch boards. "Did you have problems with him?"

Mrs. Cohn scowled. "He was too old for Emma, and Emma needed to focus on school, not a boyfriend. She'd gone on for years about going to college and getting out of here and then she's to throw it all the way on some trawl boat deckhand."

Raleigh wondered if Emma's lying had to do with her mama's disapproval.

Raleigh looked to Mike and he nodded. "Thank you for your time. We'll be in touch if we have any more questions."

Mrs. Cohn nodded before lumbering off inside, the door snapping closed behind her. Raleigh and Mike walked in silence toward the Jeep parked in the narrow driveway.

As Raleigh slid into the passenger seat, Dani appeared on the side of her.

"Jeremy's not a bad guy, you know."

Raleigh looked at her through the open door. Dani's oval face appeared innocent and weary. "Why do you say that?"

Dani shrugged, looking down at the ground. "He was just protective and stuff. Didn't want Emma doing anything stupid to ruin her life. Mama didn't like the idea of anyone caring about her more than she did. It doesn't really take much though."

Raleigh noticed a slight bitterness slip into Dani's tone, even though she smiled. "Emma and your mama had trouble?"

Dani frowned. "Not more than usual. Even though something was going on the last few weeks, but she wouldn't tell me. I overheard lots of whispering and once on the phone she said, 'I'm going to tell someone.'"

Raleigh perked up. That sounded promising. "Was that all you heard?"

Dani shrugged. "Emma and I weren't very close anymore. When we were younger, we would play together, but then she began arguing with mama and daddy and she ignored me." Tears moistened her eyes, but she blinked them away.

"Well, if you think of anything else that you heard or saw, just give me a call. It doesn't matter how small you think it is." Raleigh pulled a card from her pocket and handed it over. "If you need anything, my number is on here."

Dani accepted the card, turned and began walking down the narrow black top street. Raleigh supposed Lindsey lived in that direction. Dani appeared to be about thirteen, and Raleigh guessed—not from experience—that this would be old enough to go off on one's own. She didn't know if that would be okay with her if her other daughter had died only three days before. They hadn't even buried Emma yet, as the body hadn't been released.

Raleigh closed the door and looked to Mike. "Something was going on."

Mike nodded. "Getting teenagers to talk will be near impossible."

Especially when they didn't trust you.

"It's Monday morning," Raleigh said. "Let's see if the police are willing to release a statement, and I'll get Lathan to send us a list of all of Emma's friends."

Mike backed out of the driveway, barely missing a mailbox. "The funeral may be this week sometime."

Raleigh nodded but didn't respond. Funerals meant graveyards. Graveyards meant plenty of dead people clamoring for the small space in her head. She typically avoided the area, but it seemed she continued being invited back. Maybe that was another area she'd need to learn to deal with, like being around muddy water since she lived back in Barbeaux Bayou.

Raleigh's cellphone rang its familiar chords. She fiddled with the notebook and candy wrappers she'd tossed on the floorboards and unearthed the phone on its third ring.

Madison.

"Do I want to go on a date with Federico Taylor?"

Raleigh exhaled. Etiquette, her sister had none.

Federico Taylor was the wealthy son of local shipbuilding legend, and the direct competition of the father of Madison's son. How Madison attracted these men, Raleigh did not know. Well, maybe she did know, but she didn't want to think about it.

"I don't know," Raleigh said, smoothing out the crumpled edges of her notebook. "Do you?"

"Ugh," Madison growled. "I don't know! He's attractive. And rich, but Jefferey will work himself into a tantrum."

"Does that matter?"

"Unfortunately, yes," Madison said exasperated. "He dropped the custody case, but who knows what he will do if he gets angry. He thinks we should be a family."

Poor Madison. Two men wanted her when Raleigh couldn't tell if even one man wanted to date her or not.

"It's just a date," Raleigh said. "You aren't marrying Federico, and if Jeffery gets angry, tell him you're trying to figure out what you want."

Silence greeted her.

"That's good," Madison said, a little more energy in her voice. "I'm going to use that."

"Was there anything else?"

"Oh," Madison said quickly. "I'm going to need a favor from you. Drop by the new place to talk to me."

She hung up then.

Raleigh stared at the phone. Favors for Madison were never good. She felt dread flip-flop in her stomach.

EIGHT

Propped against the throw pillows of her tan flowered sofa, Raleigh flipped through the glossy pages of a magazine and considered the merits of fashion. An expert she was not. She wore the same black boots until the heels wore out, and then she'd buy another pair in the same name brand and color. Sheri regularly called her hair a mess and attempted to fix it every time she stepped into the shop for their Wednesday lunch dates. Aunt Clarice loved to keep these glossies around, and she claimed that to feel beautiful one had to know what beauty looked like. Raleigh supposed she knew what it looked like, but she didn't think it was her.

Glancing over at Aunt Clarice's favorite chair, Raleigh watched her great aunt's spirit flip through the latest issue of Vogue that Raleigh had picked up this weekend at the checkout counter. With the woman's pin up curls and asymmetrical collar on her shift dress, she looked as if she could have walked out of the pages of her glossy.

For how worldly the woman had been during her corporal life, one would think she'd also want a *Newsweek* or *L'Express*. Those Raleigh could relate to.

"Remember my friend Rosaline I mentioned the other day?" Aunt Clarice flipped a page casually without looking at Raleigh.

Sipping from her glass of wine, Raleigh contemplated swallowing the rest of the glass. Aunt Clarice's friends would have to be dead, and the thought of more ghosts slinking around the area made Raleigh nervous.

Aunt Clarice pursed her lips. "She's having trouble with her granddaughter." At least tonight the woman appeared in the age Raleigh remembered her instead of the twenty-something beauty that Aunt Clarice preferred.

"What kind of trouble?" Regret immediately filled Raleigh. She felt the opening for Aunt Clarice to walk right in.

Aunt Clarice patted at her curls. "Well now, she hasn't been too clear on the specifics. More like, she's been hinting that she'd like to get a message across." Aunt Clarice smiled. "Darlin', you've made waves in my world, and everyone's clamoring to talk to you."

Raleigh cringed. "Don't I know it." Even though Emma was her first murder in a month, the death rate in the area seemed to be on the rise or at least her rate of connection to the dying was on a rise. After three drug overdoses in the last month, she'd become interested in writing a story on the issue in their community, although David hadn't yet agreed to print it. The official word from the sheriff was that the town did not have a drug problem.

The dinging doorbell startled Raleigh from her thoughts.

"Oh, dear." Aunt Clarice fanned herself with her magazine, her eyes wide. "Tonight was supposed to be our quiet night."

Raleigh stood, scanning the living room with its wooden floors, white walls, and overstuffed furniture. She hadn't cleaned, but Aunt Clarice liked a straightened room on their Sunday night visits, so there was that hurried picking up before her arrival. "I'm not expecting anyone." Walking to the front door, she saw the outline of a wispy frame through the French door window.

The neighbor.

Damn.

Raleigh glanced behind her, but figured it was too late to pretend she wasn't home. With the old raised floors, her footsteps would have echoed outside, and that's if she hadn't seen her shadow through the beveled French glass. With one hand on the doorknob, she hesitated again. Breathing deeply, she cursed her family upbringing that had taught her not to be rude.

On the other side of the door, Amber stood in a flowery kaftan, her bleach blonde hair in a messy bun on the top of her head. She clutched a basket of items to her middle and her bare arms were flexed with the effort.

"Oh, I'm so glad you're home." Amber smiled, the far away gaze in her eyes sharpening a moment. "I've come to do that reading I promised."

Looking down at the basket, Raleigh now noticed the candles and tarot cards among other items. The two had spoken about this weeks ago. Meaning Amber had expressed interest and Raleigh had made noncommittal uh-huhs.

"Did we make plans?" Raleigh tried to remember if she'd nodded at the wrong time.

"Oh, no," Amber said, her laugh a bell chime. "I could feel it in the air, you know? The smell of the breeze changed, and I thought tonight would be a great night to read the cards."

Standing in the doorway, Aunt Clarice chuckled. "Let her do it. We can see if she's crazy or a real psychic."

Raleigh nodded. "Come on in."

Standing to the side, Raleigh allowed Amber to pass through the French door, noticing her wispy figure wasn't wearing undergarments under her opaque, flowery dress. If the two were close friends, Raleigh might ask her why she had a dislike for the items, but they hadn't reached that level of acquaintance yet.

Back in the living room, Raleigh removed the magazines from the coffee table and returned them to the inn table near Aunt Clarice's chair. Amber kneeled down next to the wooden table and began pulling items from the basket. Candles, matches, a cloth, cards all spilled forth and she arranged the items in some order in her head as she adjusted candles and pulled others out until she had it just so. Aunt Clarice settled into her chair, peering at the young woman with one plucked eyebrow raised.

Amber lit a candle and scanned the room. "The energy in your home is so strong it tingles my arms."

Aunt Clarice leaned back in her chair, her head nestled in the corner. "The girl may feel my presence, or she could just be a nut. Difficult to tell."

"So were you born being able to feel this energy?" Raleigh agreed with Aunt Clarice, but she approached with caution, as many would believe Raleigh herself was a nut.

Amber's eyes lost focus as she rubbed her fingers against a well-worn deck of oversized cards. "Maybe at six or seven I became aware that I was different. I saw colors surrounding people. I didn't learn until I was much older about auras. To everyone I was just the weird kid that they avoided, and I suppose I may still be." She smiled and looked right into Raleigh.

Raleigh watched her rub her cards, and she was reminded of Me'Maw. Me'Maw had a set of old playing cards on the kitchen table worn soft from her fingertips. She'd always claimed that the cards were only a tool to channel what she saw. Perhaps Amber had learned the same technique.

Aunt Clarice flicked her fingers in the air. "She's certainly a strange cookie."

Glaring at Aunt Clarice, Raleigh attempted to focus on Amber. "Everyone has something that makes them different."

Amber spread the cards out along the edges of the table. "Choose seven cards." She then looked up at Raleigh with wide eyes. "I've heard about what you can do. I sensed the ethereal when I first met you."

Aunt Clarice tsked. "Yet she can't see me here. I don't know, Chickee."

Raleigh selected her cards and handed them over to Amber, who lay them out one by one in a cross shaped arrangement on the table.

Raleigh's throat scratched. "It depends on who you heard it from whether or not it's true."

Amber laughed, a soft, sultry sound. Her unpolished nails rested on the cards. "If someone isn't saying something bad about you, you aren't living life right."

"That's the first thing she said all night that I can agree with." Aunt Clarice inspected her fingernails for any chips in the red polish as she gave Amber a side look.

Raleigh glared at the older woman. "Aunt Clarice, it's difficult to have a conversation with you commenting on everything,"

Aunt Clarice's thin eyebrow rose as a smug smile painted her perfectly tinted lips.

A weight dropped through Raleigh's chest as Aunt Clarice's triumph registered. She'd spoken aloud to someone who wasn't supposed to be there.

Amber searched the room, her eyes lingering over the chair the corner opposite Aunt Clarice. "Are we not alone? I've always wished to see a ghost or a spirit."

Raleigh coughed against the dryness in her throat. "I apologize. Seeing a spirit isn't all you think when you have no control over the spirit."

Raleigh frowned at Aunt Clarice, who stuck her chin in the air and curled her lips into a mischievous grin. "My aunt still lives in the house, even though her address is the cemetery. Sunday nights are her time to sit with the living as she calls it."

Amber nodded, her eyes still darting around the room. "Is that usual for you? I mean having ghosts as visitors?"

Raleigh laughed but then coughed again. Her throat constricted against an irritating dryness.

Raleigh glanced at Aunt Clarice who was avoiding her now. "Aunt Clarice is my only regular visitor, and I'd prefer to keep it that way."

Amber flipped over a card, laying it face up on the table. The three of clubs stared up at them. "Hmph."

Raleigh leaned forward in her seat. "What does that mean?"

"In your past you had bad luck."

Raleigh resisted the urge to roll her eyes, but a strong hint of smoke reached her nostrils, capturing her attention.

Raleigh stood, looking around the room. "Do you smell that?"

Amber looked up, startled. "What?"

"Smoke, as if something's burning."

Seeing no signs of smoke in the living room, Raleigh walked out into the hall, inspecting the ceilings and walls. Her inspection led her to the kitchen where the bottle of wine sat on the counter where she'd left it. The stove or any of the other devices that didn't get much use were not shooting out sparks or billows of smoke.

The odor clung heavily to her nostrils though.

"My house isn't on fire, dearie," Aunt Clarice spoke from behind her.

Raleigh opened a closet to reveal only linen and cleaning agents. "Are you sure?"

"Quite," Aunt Clarice said, frowning. "I'd know."

Mike. She needed to call Mike.

A compulsion to seek Mike out overwhelmed her, rattling her nerves. She knew better than to ignore the siren call.

She rushed to the living room in search of her cellphone.

Amber hovered over the cards but looked up as Raleigh ruffled through the sofa throw pillows unearthing her phone. "Everything okay?"

Raleigh dialed Mike. "Just give me a moment."

On the other end, the phone clicked, and a rustle sounded in her ear.

"Sorry, Ree," Mike said, his voice slow. "I drifted off to sleep and Trae didn't wake me."

Trae, Mike's nephew, spent Sunday nights with his uncle in order to have quality male time. He lived in a house of females with Mike's mom and half-sister and shared a room with three sisters.

Raleigh's heartbeat increased as her anxiety rocketed. "Is everything alright over there?"

"I think so," Mike said. A rustle had Raleigh's body humming over the phone. "Trae? Where are you, buddy?"

"Uncle Mike!" Trae screeched from somewhere beyond the phone speaker.

Another rustling over the phone, and a thud sounded as if the phone had fallen. Raleigh began to perspire.

"Shit, "Mike swore. "The house's on fire."

Raleigh felt her lungs bursting, unable to inhale. "I'm on my way."

NINE

Fire trucks blocked the narrow street, so Raleigh pulled her car off the road at Mike's mother's house as much as she could and set off on foot. As she cleared the house, flames licked the black sky. Breaking into a jog, she passed the neighbors huddled on the lawn gazing at the blaze.

Coughing against the thick heaviness of the air, Raleigh stopped short when she reached the front of Mike's shotgun home. The farthest side of the house was completely engulfed in flames.

On the front lawn, Teresa, Mike's mom, clutched Trae against her chest, her blue-matted, terrycloth robe wrapped round the two of them.

Raleigh approached the two, noticing Ms. Teresa's red-rimmed, puffy eyes. "Where's Mike?"

She gasped, fresh tears spilling over. "He went around back."

Darting toward the side area, a fireman rolling out a long hose yelled at her. She continued on, searching through the smoke for Mike's face.

Avoiding the bucket and hose that lay in her path by leaping in an ungraceful move, she emerged through the haze just as Mike burst out of the back door his jacket partially covering his mouth and his arms filled with items.

Chocking on the air, Raleigh rushed toward him, yanking him away from the pillowing smoke pluming from the back screen door.

Anger heated through her body, increasing the warmness from the heat of the house. "What are you doing?"

Mike's lungs heaved with the effort to expel the smoke, and he bent over with his reddened face.

Cornering the house, a fireman barreled toward them. "I need you two to come with me."

Mike attempted to straighten up but keeled over in a coughing fit again. Raleigh grabbed some of the items from his hands as he teetered upon collapse.

The fireman motioned them away from the house. "Let's get him checked out."

Walking together, Raleigh lugging a plastic container and Mike clutching his laptop to his chest, Raleigh felt the heat from the flame burning her backside and she couldn't help but think of how things could have gone differently. She couldn't look at the house again though. All she could think about is if she hadn't smelled smoke, sensed that something was wrong. She didn't even want to question right now how that had worked. From Mike's watery far-off gaze, the shock had set in and he wouldn't be asking for a while.

When they came around the front, Teresa and Trae rushed toward them. Teresa gripped her son in a tight embrace, her blue robe flapping about. She pulled when he dissolved into another coughing fit and fixed him with mother's concerned eyes.

The fireman motioned again, leading Mike toward an ambulance parked near the fire truck. "Over here."

Raleigh rubbed her hand over Trae's head, feeling his coarse hair against her flesh. "No one else was in the house, right?"

He shook his head, staring off at his Uncle Mike with big brown eyes.

Teresa pulled Trae toward her. "The others are at my house with Gina. Trae here was playing video games when Mike fell asleep."

Trae mumbled, "Uncle Mike knew what to do."

Raleigh rumpled his hair again. "Of course he did." Trae looked up at her with a conspiratorial smile.

Raleigh walked toward the ambulance, and Teresa and Trae trailed behind her.

"How's he doing?" Raleigh asked the EMT hovering over Mike, checking his blood pressure and pulse.

The EMT motioned for him to inhale from the oxygen mask. "He needs to come into the hospital for monitoring, but he's sounding better already."

"I'm doing better than my house," Mike mumbled from the plastic mask.

"That's what matters." Raleigh set the plastic container down on the edge of the ambulance.

RALEIGH STILL COULDN'T LOOK BACK at the house. From the crackling and the shouting, she didn't think the efforts were going well.

"Where are you going to live now, Uncle Mike?" Trae climbed up into the ambulance to sit next to his uncle. His big eyes fixated on the mask.

Teresa's lips straightened. "Don't worry, Trae. We'll make room for him."

Trae smiled, snuggling up close to Mike until they were touching. "I'll share my bed with you Uncle Mike. It's more comfortable than the lumpy sofa."

In Teresa's small three-bedroom house, his sister and her four children burst at the seams. All the children shared one room while his sister and her boyfriend resided in another. Mike would need to take up residence on the sofa because there was no spare inch in that house, and besides, Teresa didn't need to take in another houseguest.

The crow's feet around her eyes and the gray hairs around her temple spoke of the stress of too many mouths in one house as it was.

"He'll stay with me," Raleigh said.

"Are you sure?" Mike removed the mask from his mouth and looked at her through watery, red eyes.

Raleigh shrugged. "I have the spare bedroom available, and now I'll have a reason to clear it out."

Mike nodded as the EMT covered his mouth with the mask again.

"Great," Teresa said, looking relieved.

"Ahh, man," Trae said, his entire face darkening with his frown. "It would have been cool to have Uncle Mike instead of all the girls."

"Well, buddy," Raleigh said, knocking him on his knee. "You'll have to stick to cool sleepovers instead."

"That's not the same," he said, his face relaxing as he thought about it. "But I'll take it."

With his hat in his hand, a fireman approached. Vaguely recognizing his face, Raleigh felt as though she'd seen him before. In Barbeaux it was possible she'd seen him at the hardware store since the department worked on a volunteer basis only.

"Mike," he said, with his hand out.

"Conrad." Mike allowed the EMT to take his pulse again, but he continued his assessment of the firefighter.

Conrad Adams. Football player and all-around troublemaker. They'd attended high school with the freckled, red-haired, now smeared with soot face.

"We've nearly got the fire under control, but it will be some time before it is fully extinguished. We're taking care of the small pockets as we speak. Unfortunately, since your house is old and quite small, the fire spread quickly into the attic. I don't know how much will be salvageable."

Teresa clutched her mouth in her hand, crying. "They could have been inside that house."

Trae jumped from his seat next to Mike on the ambulance and

clung to his grandmother's side. It appeared more for her comfort than for his.

The fireman fiddled with his hat in his hands. "We've called in the inspector, but it's safe to say that it's arson. The accelerant left a trail across the posterior wall and into the grass. There wasn't an attempt to hide it."

"Oh," Teresa cried out again, clutching Trae tighter.

"What happens now?" Mike asked, his face blank.

"Like I said, there will be an investigation."

Conrad walked away, his helmet hanging in his hands.

"I'll call Joey." Thoughts raced through her head. Someone had intentionally tried to burn down the house with Mike and Trae inside.

Jeremy had acted strangely earlier, but why would he burn down Mike's house? It's not as if Mike and Raleigh knew anything about Emma's death.

But if it weren't him, who was it? Did they have some other loose cannon running around?

TEN

The tall, top-heavy principal strolled toward her with a walkie-talkie in one hand and a clipboard in another. With wavy blond hair and a peacock feather-patterned scarf around her neck, she appeared fashionably all business.

Her brow crinkled with her slight smile as she came to a stop in front of Raleigh. "The students will be excited."

Pushing the load of school newspapers on the dolly, Raleigh stopped in the middle of the main hall. "The students worked hard on this, and I'm glad we were able to help."

Her walkie-talkie crackled, and her hand lifted it to her face. "Tell them I will be by shortly to take a peek. I just need to drop in on this administrative meeting first."

She continued down the hall, barking directions into the walkie-talkie.

Raleigh steered the dolly haphazardly down the hall until she stood before Lathan Babin's journalism classroom. Typically, she'd leave heavy lifting jobs to Mike, but he'd taken today off to get the insurance and fire marshal reports straight. He'd looked haggard this morning with dark splotches under his eyes and a general weariness weighing his shoulders down. She hated that she couldn't be there today, but someone had to carry out Tuesday's tasks.

Raleigh knocked and the tall brunette, who played soccer and didn't speak much in class when the school had first approached them about printing a physical paper copy of their news, opened the door for her. His other classmates turned toward the door and big smiles lit up the room as they focused on the cart of papers. Raleigh had thought they were going in the wrong direction. This, after all, was the online social media generation, but seeing one's name in print hadn't skipped this generation of instant gratification. The students had worked diligently, following the guidelines she and Mike had come in periodically to explain. With this second edition, the students had worked out some of their differences in opinions over layout, and Raleigh thought this one had a more aesthetic appearance.

According to their reaction today, their excitement hadn't dulled yet even with the work involved.

Mr. Babin walked from the back of the room, standing out from the students by only his worn blazer and wrinkled shirt. "We were just speaking about you, waiting anxiously for your arrival, of course."

Keith and Dex stepped forward and retrieved the cart from Raleigh, pulling it toward the middle of the classroom. Raleigh followed them in, approaching Lathan. A few desks littered the middle of the room, but a majority of the room was overwhelmed with a green screen against the back wall and a side wall lined with computer stations.

Raleigh said, "It's challenging without my sidekick today."

"How's he handling this ordeal?" Lathan asked. "The hits just keep coming."

His eyes slid over his students, who congregated over the crate of newspapers except for a group of three students who huddled together disregarding the rest of the class.

"The emergency room cleared him at some awful hour last

night," Raleigh said. "He's taking care of the unfortunate details today of salvaging what is left."

"Awful, I'm sure," Lathan said. "Everyone's feeling terrible today. I've been building up the excitement of the paper to bring up the mood, and it has worked for some."

Raleigh scanned the room and could see the tempered excitement as they flipped through their eight-page issue. "I'm sure Emma's absence from the class has made daily life difficult."

The red-haired beauty Olivia turned around. "Difficult? It's terrible. Unimaginable. I've tried texting her a hundred times but then I remember I can't, and it hits all over again. It's unbearable."

Raleigh remembered that the few times she'd dealt with Emma, Olivia had been attached, finishing her sentences. "I'm so sorry."

"At least I make myself wake up and come to school." A tear traveled down her cheek, trailing through a layer of contour and highlighter. "Jeremy hasn't been at school since Thursday. He can't face it."

"Really?" So none of the friends at school knew that Jeremy was avoiding police questioning. He was simply the crushed boyfriend.

Olivia nodded. "He's devasted, and Mrs. Cohn may not let him go to the funeral so he's crumbling."

"She doesn't really like Jeremy, does she?" Raleigh said. "Did something happen to cause so much dislike?"

Olivia shrugged. "Mrs. Cohn had this idea about what Emma's life should be like, and it didn't include a guy without a future. Truthfully, I think Mrs. Cohn wanted to make sure Emma had a career that provided the family money. That was just my impression."

Raleigh didn't know much about Jeremy or what kind of person he was. For instance, was he the type to set someone's house on fire when he was angry? Raleigh hoped not, but the evidence dealing with him thus far spoke of a temper and a possessive nature. Emotional trauma could be the cause for both of these though, so she didn't want to form a hasty opinion of the teenager. From her meeting with Mrs. Cohn, she'd felt a mother's grief, though maybe the woman had had questionable moments as well. All subjective she knew, as Raleigh had only spent fifteen minutes with the woman at most. So perhaps she needed to consider what Max used to refer to as hard evidence instead of just her subjective instinct. This would mean she'd need to acquire some—evidence that is.

Lathan led her away from Olivia by the elbow, "Would you be willing to attend a faculty social? I figure with all the time spent here the past month, you've become part of the staff. The socials aren't too bad and are usually at a restaurant where we can finally have that drink I've been promising you guys."

"The staff has these socials often?" Raleigh couldn't tell if the invitation included Mike or just her. A week ago, he'd barely paid her any mind, but twice now he'd thrown her off with an invitation.

He grinned, a dimple appearing on his left cheek. "Twice a year. Christmas and the annual fundraiser. Both pretty fun."

"Why don't you send me the details, and I'll check my schedule."

More like she'd check Mike's schedule. She didn't believe accepting a date from Lathan Babin or even giving him the idea that it was a date was a good idea. His reputation didn't include her type, and besides, she didn't want to send the wrong message to Mike. If Mike was paying attention at all, which she couldn't tell either. Maybe she needed to get dating advice.

His grin deepened. "Great."

Principal Rodrigue slipped into the room and the students clamored to show her the new issue. Raleigh used the opportunity to slip out. The students handled the paper delivery process, and they'd share the school's reaction when it was time to work on the next issue. After the initial start-up, Barbeaux Gazette's involvement was minimal. Soon she wouldn't need to be involved at all, as their own delivery driver was set to begin delivering to the school in a few weeks on his usual route. Raleigh would be able to fill her time with something else.

Ten minutes later she parallel parked near Madison's new venue space next door to Austin Lebasque's restaurant. Madison's silver coupe was parked right in front of the glass windows flashing a large print banner that read "Venue Coming Soon." Austin had invested in Madison's newest business foray, of which Raleigh hadn't been privy to the details. In Madison's defense, Raleigh had attempted to stay uninvolved, figuring that she and her sister needed some time apart after their last venture. Playing the big sister role was tiresome to Raleigh as well as irksome for Madison.

Grabbing the files off the passenger seat, Raleigh ambled over to the door. She peeked in through the glass for signs of Madison, but the door opened when she pulled on it tentatively. Safety never seemed to enter Madison's mind.

Madison was sitting in the middle of the floor assembling some kind of shelf, her hair tied back and her jeans spotted with the same gray paint that glistened from the walls.

Madison glanced up from her construction project, focusing in on the manila files. "Oh, thank you so much. You're a lifesaver."

Raleigh scanned the empty area. At least now the walls held a coat of paint and the flooring tiles had been installed. Several paintings and décor items rested in a crate in the middle of the floor along with a few boxes that showed black and white sketches of furniture.

"It's coming along nicely," Raleigh commented, wondering how much capital Lebasque had invested. Madison's idea of investing was buying herself a new pair of shoes—the expensive kind because they lasted longer.

"I need it to go a tad quicker." Madison frowned, leaning back on her elbows. "I have the grand opening event Saturday, and I don't want to delay it."

Raleigh placed the folders down on a metal chair next to the crate. "Is that what these are?"

"No," Madison said. "Friday night I'm hosting a singles cocktail mixer at Lebasque's. We're building publicity for the venue, getting the word out and all. Austin wanted to go over the guest list for lunch, and of course, I left it home when I was reviewing it last night. If this place wasn't such a construction zone, I may actually have an office instead of a storage room right now."

"You're making it happen though." Raleigh did have to give her sister credit. Madison could create a business idea and make it happen—legal or illegal.

"I am, aren't I?" Madison grinned. "Say, about that favor. I need you to come Friday. I need single professionals, and it has been a little bit of an issue finding them. You could mix with all the upscale singles, so there would be something in it for you, too."

Raleigh wrinkled her nose. "Upscale? Not really my type."

Madison shrugged. "Who knows? You may meet someone nice. That is if you and Mike aren't together yet." She raised an eyebrow but didn't ask anything further.

Twice in the same day, no in the same hour, Raleigh had to consider if she and Mike had made some arrangement not to date other people. Mike hadn't dated anyone recently that she'd noticed, but the two of them didn't seem to be moving forward either. The question remained though; did she want to make a move like that without talking to him first?

"Besides you could possibly cover the event for the paper and provide free publicity for your sister's business." Madison wiggled her eyebrows and added a grin.

"Could that be the real reason for my invitation?" Raleigh asked.

Madison frowned. "Can't I just want my sister to come out and support me?"

Ah, yes, Madison was laying it on thick.

Fifteen minutes later, Raleigh still debated if she should be attending Madison's party. Doing a favor for Madison could cost her down the line, but perhaps if she jump-started Mike into thinking she were ready to date, he'd stop acting like everything was the same as it had been since they were four years old.

At Danny's Diner, cars filled the gravel parking lot. The old-fashioned diner's orange paint peeled under the heat of the mid-day sun. As a typical roadside diner, the place was a hidden treasure trove of the best comfort food in Barbeaux Bayou. And Raleigh's hopes were that comfort food would ease Mike's pain of the day.

The bell jangled Raleigh's entrance, but with the cacophony of the voices no one would hear the announcement. The five o'clock crowd had filled the booths and tables with Barbeaux Bayou's older generation who ate at this time daily. Typically, Raleigh could say hello to Me'Maw and Paw's friends as she picked up her take-out at least once a week.

At the counter, she didn't see Max until she was nearly right on top of him. She smiled but allowed her eyes to slide over him to Cindy behind the counter.

Cindy popped her pink gum. "Hun, your order will be a few minutes since the kitchens swamped. Sorry."

Raleigh noticed the phone from the back wall resting off the hook on the counter. She'd suspected the busy signal often had nothing to do with call volume.

"No problem," Raleigh said. "Can I get a root beer while waiting?"

"Sure, hun." Cindy pulled a Styrofoam cup from under the counter and faced the large bubbling machine. The diner brewed their own root beer and served it with crushed ice pellets which equaled the sweetest concoction in Barbeaux Bayou.

"You think maybe we could talk while you're waiting?" Max paused over his half-eaten hamburger.

Raleigh did a sweep of the restaurant, but she saw no one who could get her out of this.

Raleigh slid onto the empty bar stool next to the register as Cindy set her lidded soft drink and straw on the sticky, wooden counter. "Sure."

Silence passed between them as Raleigh slipped her straw into the plastic lid. Only last month she would have reached into Max's fries and stolen one without a thought, but now she couldn't wait for her order to come up so she could escape.

Max leaned over the counter on his elbows. "I wanted to say I was sorry about how things ended."

Raleigh twirled on her stool. "I should apologize for handling it the way I did. It wasn't my finest moment."

Max shook his head. "You were right. We couldn't pretend to be other people to make it work. At the time, I just wasn't open to hearing it."

Raleigh smiled, fiddling with her Styrofoam cup. "We should have known it wouldn't work. Law enforcement doesn't mix with the Cheramie sisters."

Max tapped on the counter with his index finger and thumb. "I don't know. I think Sheriff Breaux would prefer you'd stay away more."

Raleigh shrugged. "He does make my life difficult. You'd think he'd lighten up if I'm helping him do his job."

"I think that's precisely it." Max raised an eyebrow. "You make him look bad."

Sheriff Breaux must suffer from more pride than Joey then, who took no issue with Raleigh's help. Joey cared more about solving the cold cases and giving the families answers than being outdone. Of course, Sheriff Breaux's distrust of her went all the way back to high school when he couldn't arrest her. He'd been pressured by powerful families in Barbeaux Bayou, and the embarrassment had been enough to keep an eleven-year grudge going strong.

Raleigh's phone vibrated in her pocket and she answered without a look at the screen, assuming Mike needed something or had decided to inquire about dinner.

"Raleigh, I have an interesting bit of evidence for you to look over for me," Joey said on the other end.

Glancing over at Max, she wondered if he should be privy to this conversation Sharing evidence with her probably wasn't a great way for Joey to further his career.

"You do?" She responded, the tone of her voice even.

Joey coughed. "That bracelet was a match for a missing item in a cold case file. I knew it looked familiar. I'd gone through all these files when they were turned over to me, and I'd seen the photograph before probably a dozen times."

"Really?" Raleigh asked, finding it difficult to disguise her interest. "How long ago?"

"Four years," Joey said, paper rustling in the background. "Another dead girl, about the same age actually. Bracelet's tarnished, but otherwise it's the same as reported missing."

"What's the likelihood that the bracelet is just one of many?" Raleigh asked, playing with the straw on her root beer.

"Not likely when it's engraved with a quote that the girl's mother said she lived by."

"Hmm," Raleigh said, thinking. The bracelet brought up numerous scenarios, chilling possibilities about teenage girls. Maybe Jeremy hadn't had anything to do with it after all.

"You still there?" Joey asked.

"Yes," Raleigh responded, dragging herself up from her thoughts. "Why don't you bring it over, and we can see what shakes out."

"Gotcha," Joey said, a car horn sounding in the back. "I'll see you later."

Cindy placed a white to-go bag in front of her. "Nice and hot for you, hun."

"Thanks," Raleigh said, placing cash down on the countertop.

Max cleared his throat. "I remember that case. It was one of my first homicides when I made detective."

With her hand gripping the take-out bag, Raleigh glanced over at him. She felt as if she had been caught stealing peanuts from her Paw's secret stash at eight years old.

"I guess you heard the conversation then."

Raleigh hoped Joey wouldn't take any heat for this. He'd been so happy to finally get to be detective, even it if only was for cold cases. Sheriff Breaux may bump him back down to patrol if Max went run and reveal the conversation. She should have mentioned Max was sitting next to her, given Joey the option to keep quiet.

He glanced at her with that chick of hair beginning to drift to its sticking up position. "I couldn't find any lead that would pan out. Maybe Joey will have better luck."

Something in his voice, a wistfulness maybe, told Raleigh he may not mean it. He'd wanted to solve that case.

"I'll see you around, Max." Raleigh grabbed the bag and headed out.

She needed to give Joey a warning.

ELEVEN

Tossing the keys onto the side table, Raleigh continued down the entrance following the soft thumping sound of something scraping against the floor. "Mike, I have sustenance."

From the front bedroom doorway, Mike's blond mop poked out. "I'm almost done with these boxes. I'll be there soon."

Allowing him to disappear back into the room, Raleigh continued down to the kitchen and placed the bag on the counter. Breakfast dishes cluttered the sink and a half-eaten sandwich rested on a plate at the side of the drain board. Mike had left dirty dishes and he'd held off on food, both causes for concern. Mike had brooded all day.

As she walked back down the hall toward the bedroom, she noticed the return of a painting of the Aegean Sea on the wall. Aunt Clarice had brought this home from her travels, and it had hung on the wall Raleigh's entire life. In her thirties, Aunt Clarice had embarked on a whirlwind three-month tour of Europe, something unheard of for a woman from Barbeaux Bayou at the time. This painting had been packed among the boxes of mementos Raleigh had procrastinated unpacking and sorting. In the middle of moving the boxes, Mike must have hung it on its original nail.

In the bedroom, only three boxes and the old bed frame remained. The old, antique frame crusted with peeling white paint once belonged to Aunt Clarice and had been wrapped in layers of colorful fabric.

Raleigh stepped inside. "I can see the floor."

Mike grunted, his head rising from behind the bed frame. "I brought two boxes of photographs and albums to Paw to sort through. I also shelved Aunt Clarice's record albums in the dining room, and I put up a few paintings. I left three armoire boxes for you to go through."

He continued twisting a bolt into place. His voice and face seemed dejected.

Raleigh sank to the bare wood floorboards by the door. "Were you able to salvage anything from your house?"

Another grunt in response. "Everything that isn't burnt has a smoke stench."

"I'm sorry." Raleigh didn't know what else to say to ease his anguish. She could promise to find out what happened, but fire wasn't her area of expertise. She dealt strictly with the dead.

Mike leaned back on his knees. "There's only a few items I would have wanted. You know my yearbooks, some pictures, that cap my dad brought me when I was eight. I had clothes over here, in the Jeep, and at Jeff's house, and my mom has a few pictures that I can get copies made. I just wanted a few more things, you know?"

Mike's face sagged as he stared down at the wrench in his hands.

"I'm sure your mom has something you can have from your dad." Raleigh bit down on her trembling bottom lip. Mike's dad had died when they were eight years old, and Raleigh remembered the pain in his face the morning of the funeral.

Mike shrugged, his head disappearing behind the bed frame again.

"And you see people from high school around town all the time. No need for pictures. You just need to remember that age hasn't been kind."

Raleigh smiled, hoping a stab at humor would lighten his mood, but he continued twisting at the bolt and didn't look up at her. She'd need something more than a bad joke to pull him out of his funk, not that she blamed him. Someone had set his house on fire with him inside, not to mention his nephew.

A knock came at the door, and Raleigh struggled to her feet.

"Expecting someone?" Mike leaned back on his hands, his head reappearing from behind the bed.

Raleigh paused at the doorway, meeting his eyes. Mike's easygoing spark had dulled.

"Joey's brought a cold case he thinks is connected to Emma's murder."

He raised an eyebrow. "Oh?"

Raleigh tilted her head in a sign of not knowing before continuing to the door. Mike worried about her working on cold cases for the sheriff's office, not because he didn't want her helping people, but he was leery that Sheriff Breaux could manipulate her involvement criminally and tie her to one of those cases. He and Joey's conversations revolved around protecting her from this outcome. When they got into these conversations, Raleigh could only roll her eyes. Joey kept her name out of his reports, and she thought that should cover it.

On the other side of the French doors, Cousin Joey waited with his usual John Deere cap on and an oversized manila envelope under his arm.

He grinned, his dimple in his right cheek forming. "I believe you and I need to set up an office."

She shut the door behind him and followed him into the living room where they typically crowded around, unless it was really serious, and they needed to spread out at the old, unused dining table.

"I would volunteer to convert the spare bedroom into an office, but I've rented it out to Mike now."

Mike shuffled in from the hall. "You could always convert the dining area into an office. It's not as if you use the table."

Scrunching up her nose, Raleigh sank onto Aunt Clarice's

chair. It was a chair she only sat in when company was over because you never knew when Aunt Clarice would show up. If Raleigh moved the dining room table out, Aunt Clarice would probably have a posse of ghosts carrying it back in at night—not something Raleigh wanted to hear bumping around when it was dark.

Joey placed the envelope on the coffee table. "I don't remember eating in there much when we were children. Aunt Clarice wasn't much of a cook as I remember."

The notorious woman had written her column for the Barbeaux Gazette and later on for the big city newspaper. She'd liked her Virginia Slims and her fashion magazines, and she'd pick at the dishes Me'Maw would send over for her because everyone said she was too skinny. As far as Raleigh could tell, Aunt Clarice liked being thin because she appreciated how her clothes followed her curves. In truth, there was a little bit of her in Madison—or maybe a whole handful.

As far as that dining alcove, Raleigh might enter once a week to wipe the dust off of whatever surface it clung to, but that was the extent of its use. But like she'd thought every time the idea had come up, no ghosts would be moving that table back inside while she slept.

Raleigh looked at the envelope. "So, what kind of connection do you think exists between Emma and this other girl?"

The envelope crinkled as Joey picked it up. "As far as I can tell from a preliminary search, the bracelet would be all right now. The families aren't related. The young woman was four years ahead of Emma in school. As a senior it's unlikely they knew each other except for the news when Courtney Theriot's body was discovered dumped off of Turner Road."

Sitting down on the sofa, Mike ran a hand through his shaggy blonde hair. "Any suspects at the time?"

Joey shrugged as he retrieved a delicate bracelet from a plastic bag. "The mother said there was a boyfriend, but none of her friends knew of any boyfriend. The report says that the father was a suspect briefly, but he was cleared. He died two years ago. Self-inflicted gunshot wound to the head."

Rubbing a finger along the smooth, delicate indentation in her wrist, she contemplated the bracelet Joey had set in front of her. She'd been working on this skill with her tutor, and even though her adeptness at reaching those last moments of life with an object had increased, it didn't get any easier.

Mike leaned forward, studying the tarnished bracelet. "Maybe feelings of guilt?"

Joey tilted his head in thought. "That wouldn't explain how Emma ended up with Courtney's bracelet four years after her death."

Raleigh nodded. She picked up the bracelet and slid it onto her palm. It was cold against her clammy hand. Tightening her fist around it, Raleigh closed her eyes and measured her breathing and focused on the object.

For the first minute, she felt only the cold metal and the eyes of Joey and Mike on her. With her eyes closed, she could only imagine their expectant faces, waiting for the tidbits of the connection.

Psychometry was tricky for her. Death left an impression on an object, and she could connect to death. But since Courtney Theriot's body had been found four years ago and her spirit had gone on without reaching out to Raleigh, the impression she received would only be a flash, a brief imprint. Her fear often prevented it from working as her greatest fear would be to find herself in a coffin. Since she lived the dead's last moments, she wasn't convinced it couldn't happen.

With a final calming breath, darkness swallowed her. A steady swaying to and fro nauseated her. With a jerk forward, she felt suspended in the darkness, tossed at the whim of the crashing waves or simply space.

Then it was gone.

Raleigh dropped the bracelet back on top of the plastic.

She shook her head as if trying to clear the throbbing in the center of her forehead.

"I don't know if that was Emma or Courtney." Raleigh tried to recall helpful details that she may not have recognized in the moment. "The darkness meant I couldn't see a thing, but there was plenty of movement. A general tossing about. Perhaps the back of a car?"

Joey leaned back against the back of the recliner. "It's likely both girls were transported by vehicle to their disposal site. What we need is something that ties them together."

A knock sounded on the front door.

Mike and Raleigh's eyes met, and she shrugged. Paw entered through the back door as he'd done his entire adult life, and Madison tended not to knock. Other than that, she didn't get many unannounced visitors.

Mike's long legs disappeared around the door arch and returned moments later, leading Max into the room.

Glancing toward the cold case file on the coffee table, Raleigh's temperature rose. She needed more of a warning to hide it. "What are you doing here today, Max?"

Reaching out, he handed her a folded piece of white paper. "It's an address for Eula Mae Theriot. She moved after the death of her daughter, and I thought this may be helpful."

Staring at the slip of paper, Raleigh hesitated. He'd been so cold. Why had he decided to help her now? "Why would you give me this?"

Max glanced around the room, his eyes homing in on the bracelet. "I couldn't help her four years ago, but maybe you can."

Joey remained stoically quiet. Raleigh guessed the two of them had not made up since the argument at the crime scene. Both could be stubborn in their own way.

Mike cleared his throat. "Do they have any leads on the arson at my house?"

Max didn't look toward Mike. "We are interviewing neighbors right now."

"Don't worry, Mike," Joey said. "You have plenty of good neighbors. They're good people who want to help. Someone saw someone who didn't belong there, I'm sure of it."

"I don't know," Mike said, shaking his head. "Lately, there's been too much traffic. I think a house in the back may be dealing."

Max looked at Mike, focusing on the top of his head "Well at least now you don't have to deal with the street going to snuff."

Mike grumbled "Well, I'm at Raleigh's now, but I still have to worry about my mom and sister down that street."

Max glanced at Raleigh and then back at Mike's head. "You're staying here?" Max asked, his tone leveling out.

Mike nodded.

"I'm renting him the extra bedroom," Raleigh said, wondering how long it would take Max to stop playing nice. He seemed to be reaching the edge of his line. "Of course, I have to give a discount since he actually did all the work of cleaning it out."

Max nodded, not meeting anyone's eyes. "Joey, keep me updated with the case." Max looked to Mike. "Mike, I'll let you know when we have something on the arson." His eyes slid over Raleigh. "I'll see myself out, Raleigh."

They waited until they heard the click of the door before Joey collected the bracelet and returned it to its bag. "I'm surprised he's helping us."

Mike looked at her, and Raleigh's cheeks burned under the gloomy darkening of his normally sunny disposition. He grumbled, "I'm not."

TWELVE

Raleigh scanned through Joey's notes attached to Courtney Theriot's homicide file one more time. She'd read the actual case file once, and she agreed with Joey's notes that some discrepancies existed in witness statements. She didn't know what she was hoping to cling to as they traveled toward her mother, but Raleigh found the living so much more difficult to deal with than the dead. Joey's neat print spelled out that every lead had been a dead end and the physical evidence nonexistent after the body had been submerged in the canal for four days before it was found by a local trapper. When Courtney had disappeared, never returning home from a night out at a friend's house, she'd been wearing the bracelet, but it had never been discovered.

So how had Emma come into possession of the same bracelet?

Four years ago when Courtney had died, Raleigh had been living in Texas closing herself off to her connection to the dead. She'd wanted to forget everything about her ability and the bayou then. Now, she didn't think she could close herself off if she tried.

Joey cleared his throat and Raleigh looked over at him in the driver's seat. "Talk is that her mom doesn't like Sheriff Breaux."

Raleigh shuffled the pages back into the folder. "We can bond over our mutual dislike. Do we know why?"

Joey shrugged, his lips thinning to a straight line. He'd never speak ill of the sheriff although he disliked the man as much as everyone else in the family.

Raleigh placed the folder on the back seat and looked at Joey as she turned to do so. "My guess would be that she didn't appreciate the way that Sheriff Breaux handled the case."

Joey signaled to merge into the next lane. "To tell you the truth, I wish someone would run against him in this election. Eleven years as sheriff, and thirty-six years of his influence on the department has been enough, I think."

"Do you think others feel the same way?"

Joey said, "Some. There's always that good ol' boys club that wants to keep him in his position. Breaux does plenty favors for a select few, but someone new might mean you and I could work openly together."

Joey hadn't been honest with his sergeant when he'd left the station to drive down and interview this Eula Mae Theriot, Courtney's mother. They knew his location and intentions, but they did not know Raleigh would be present. Joey didn't like being dishonest, but he took these cold cases personal. He believed that if the case could have closure or justice, Raleigh should be able to have a go at it. No stone left unturned and all that cliché nonsense. Playing super-heroes when they were children had always been his idea. He'd wanted to save people and bring justice even back then when they didn't know what the bad guys were truly capable of doing. This was what made Joey the man he was—a version with morals instilled by Paw.

Raleigh rubbed the scar on her wrist. "You should run for sheriff, Joey."

"Nah," Joey said. "No one would vote for me. I don't have a name for myself."

"Sure they would," Raleigh said. "Everyone knows our family—

the good and bad. You've been on the force since you were eighteen, and people actually like you."

"I'm young," he said, shaking his head. "Everyone will say that I need more experience."

"Then you tell them you will draw from the experience of the best Barbeaux has to offer. You can stress that we need a change."

Joey looked through the windshield, his lips and eyebrows twitching as he studied the blacktop before them, but really, he thought about what Raleigh had proposed. Getting Sheriff Breaux out of office would be the ultimate strategy in preventing him from trying to arrest her for every dying person who made a connection and wanted her help. For other unselfish reasons though, it would also be a great move for Joey. At eight years old, he'd pinned that shiny plastic sheriff's badge from the dime store on his flannel shirt and worn it everywhere. He'd wanted this since the first time he'd met the sheriff at the local festival.

Glancing her way with a glint in his eye, Joey nodded. "I just may consider it. I'll have to talk it over with Sue Ann first as she'd have to live with it, too."

Raleigh smiled. She just may be able to make this happen. With a quick chat with Sue Ann, Raleigh could change the circumstances of the Cheramies. Sue Ann could certainly be persuaded.

Two minutes later, Joey pulled his cruiser into the cement driveway of a brick house resembling every other house on the street. After a quick survey of the street, Raleigh surmised that the neighborhood had four styles of houses with only slight variations in brick colors or neutral paint schemes on the front siding. Within the last five years, this subdivision of fifty houses had been thrown up to accommodate the growing families who wanted newer homes. The subdivision consisted of three streets with houses in various states of development. Located on the outskirts of town limits, Raleigh wondered if the open cow pastures they'd passed would also become cookie cutter houses. With small town, rural life becoming more appealing to people, Raleigh suspected that this neighborhood would explode.

Clutching an overstuffed calico cat staring at them with uninterested eyes, Eula Mae Theriot answered the door in a flowy, large purple tulip kaftan that floated around her skeletal frame.

Sucking in until her cheekbones protruded, Eula Mae led them silently into an airy living room area. Dumping the cat unceremoniously onto a love seat, she motioned for Joey and Raleigh to sit on a tattered white sofa. Looking at the cat stretching and sinking its claws into the cushion, Raleigh suspected the cat was responsible for the rips on the side of the sofa.

"Sandals!" Eula Mae exclaimed.

Looking at her disinterested one last time, the cat jumped down and disappeared around the corner.

Eula Mae sank onto the chair. "It was my daughter's cat." She frowned. "I can't bear to get rid of it, but it has destroyed everything in my house."

Joey nodded. "We're here about your daughter's case."

"Oh, Sheriff Breaux decided she didn't runaway?" The bitterness in Eula Mae's voice crawled into the corners of the room and scratched at the floor.

Joey stood, hands in pockets, brow furrowed. "I'm in charge of cold cases now." Raleigh felt as though she'd missed something in the exchange. Joey had held something back about Sheriff Breaux's involvement, but Raleigh could figure it out later.

Joey maintained eye contact with Eula Mae. "Recently, your daughter's bracelet turned up on another victim's body, which has brought your daughter's file to my attention."

Eula Mae stared off to a spot above their heads, her eyes unfocused. "I don't know what else I can tell you about my daughter. I knew she hadn't run away because she wouldn't do that to me."

Raleigh had no experience on the parent's perspective of losing a child, but she had plenty experience with being the victim and not being believed.

"At the time you told police that she left the house that day with the bracelet," Raleigh said. "Are you sure or could it possibly have been lost prior to that day?"

Eula Mae turned golden, deep reflective eyes on her. "No, I had to fix the clasp for her because it had been bent. Her sister Sarah put it on her wrist before she went out."

Joey's knee knocked against a glass coffee table and he retreated further into the seat. "And she told you it was from her boyfriend?"

Eula Mae rolled her eyes. "Look, I know what they said in those reports about her making it up, but there was a boyfriend."

The notes in the report had concluded after questioning friends, relatives, and school officials that there was no boyfriend. The general consensus of Max and the sheriff had been that Courtney had made the boyfriend up to get out of the house to hide whatever activity she was into that caused her death. The trouble with this notion was that no trace of this activity had been found either. Joey had highlighted this in his own notes.

Raleigh glanced down at the file under her folded hands. "Do you remember anything about this boyfriend that could help us figure out who he was?"

Eula Mae shrugged her boney shoulders, a clavicle jutting through the bathrobe. "She said she wasn't ready to tell me who he was. She and I argued about it, but she was headstrong and stubborn." She laughed, a coarse, rough sound. "I trusted her. I believed she'd be alright."

Raleigh nodded, offering a sympathetic smile of encouragement.

Tears sprung to Eula Mae's eyes. "I'm not a bad mother."

"No, of course not," Joey said, fiddling with his cap. "We all do the best we can. Now that I have something to go on, I'm going to try and figure out what happened."

Eula Mae stared into Raleigh's eyes and Raleigh hardened her spine in preparation of what was to come. "I know who you are."

Raleigh bit down on her bottom lip. News of her connecting to the dead had made it around town with each family she'd worked with. Me'Maw had a reputation as traiteur, and it wouldn't take long for Raleigh's name to follow. She hadn't worked out how she felt about that yet.

Eula Mae rose. "Let me show you something." Raleigh followed her to a corner curio cabinet, one of the only solid pieces of furniture in the room besides a short entertainment center in the sitting area.

On the top of the cabinet, she switched on a light switch and the items of a child lit up from within the darkness.

"These are Courtney's things." Eula Mae exhaled; the sound filled with melancholy. "I couldn't hold onto everything of course, but these were the things she thought were important."

Within a case, a journal with beat up blue leather stood tall, leaning against the back glass, a frosted mug with Barbeaux High Prom engraved stood next to the journal, and framed photographs of a pretty brunette with various friends dotted the shelves. A shriveled-up corsage sat in the corner as if it knew no one should touch it or it could fall apart.

Raleigh stared through the glass, thinking of all the times Courtney would have touched the items. "Can I touch something?" Truthfully Raleigh didn't know if she wanted to try this in front of someone unfamiliar with the process. Eula Mae might have heard about her, but hearing and seeing brought a different level of reaction in people.

Eula Mae seemed to sense this impending strangeness. She remained still breathing heavily onto the glass, staring into her daughter's mementos. Then she gave a slight nod.

Reaching out, Raleigh opened the delicate clasp of the door and brushed her fingers against the dry, brittle flowers. The petals felt rough, devoid of moisture against her fingertips. Touching those would take her back to a moment in Courtney's life when she knew happiness.

Raleigh clasped her fingers around the pick with its silver hand ban folded under it. The shelves evaporated before her, and she stood on a front porch, looking out at a cracked sidewalk and unmowed lawn A tall figure came up behind her and tousled her hair. She laughed and looked into Jeremy's face. A much younger and relaxed face. His hair longer and his cheeks fluffier from baby fat.

"You're too grown up for me now," Jeremy grinned. "Watch out!"

Reaching up, she patted her hair, checking for hairs out of place in her updo. "You can't mess up the hair. That's what being grown up means, you know?"

"Nah," Jeremy said, his eyes shining. "It means you get all fancy. Hair, flowers, a dress. What next? You become a movie star and forget us little people?"

She laughed, blushing. "Oh, Jeremy, I'll never leave you behind." She looked toward a blue sports car with tinted windows pulling into the front drive. "Well, here I go. Wish me luck."

Jeremy grinned. "You don't need it."

She smiled wide and turned and ran off to the driveway toward the waiting car, her two-inch heels clacking along the cement.

Pulling her hand away from the coarse flowers, Raleigh steadied herself against the cabinet.

Eula Mae's eyes were widened. "What happened?"

Raleigh shook the vestige of the memory away, so she could focus. "How did your daughter know Jeremy Garcia?"

"They were cousins," Eula Mae said, her voice cracking with emotion. "Why?"

"He's the boyfriend of our recent victim who had Courtney's bracelet," Joey said. He stood near the sofa with his arms crossed across his chest.

"Something's not right then." Eula Mae shook her head. "Those two were extremely close, like brother and sister. I'm sure Jeremy hasn't done anything wrong."

Raleigh clamped down on her bottom lip. She wanted to believe Jeremy hadn't done anything wrong either, but evidence was piling up against him.

"When did Courtney receive the bracelet?"

"For her birthday," Eula Mae said, shuffling back toward the sofa.

"She told me it was a present from her boyfriend, and then three weeks later she was missing."

Raleigh nodded. Instinct and experience told her that this bracelet would unlock this case. They needed to discover what they could about where this bracelet had come from and how both victims had come to have it nearly four years apart.

After promising to keep her updated, Joey and Raleigh headed back to town so she could retrieve her car at the Barbeaux Gazette to meet Sheri for their standing Wednesday lunch date.

Joey signaled a right turn back onto the main highway and glanced over at Raleigh. "Why would a young girl hide a boyfriend's identity?"

Raleigh chewed on her bottom lip, contemplating the question. In high school, Raleigh had never had an occasion to lie about a boyfriend as she hadn't dated much. Madison might know a thing or two about hiding things as she'd had an entire secret life.

"The boy may be someone the family doesn't approve of. We'd need to know Eula Mae's prejudices to narrow that one down. Or, it could be an older man that she feared introducing to her mom."

Joey nodded, considering her answer. "Possibly someone in the family? Like a cousin?"

Raleigh winced. Jeremy and Courtney were cousins, and Jeremy had been at least three years younger. He did seem to admire her though.

Raleigh's cellphone rang, and she reached for it in her bag under the file. The screen read Mike.

Putting him on speakerphone, she and Joey greeted him together.

"Me'Maw called to remind us about dinner tonight," Mike said, sounding distracted.

Raleigh groaned. "I completely forgot about dinner."

Joey chuckled. "You two don't want to miss that or that woman will chase you with a newspaper."

Raleigh laughed, but she noticed Mike's silence from the other side of the line.

"I'll be home in time," Raleigh said, ending the phone call.

"Mike will come around," Joey said. "He just needs to figure out his place again. He's lived in that house since he came back from college."

Raleigh nodded as she stared out the passenger window watching the trees and old building go by. She felt as though she should be able to help him through this. He'd always managed to figure out what she needed, but she didn't have a clue right now how to ease this for him.

Hopefully, some of Me'Maw's home cooking tonight could elicit at least some response.

Twenty minutes later the bell above the door signaled her entrance into Sheri's shop. Running late, she'd avoided going into the office and having someone stop her. She'd pick up notes for the story on the lawsuit against the town over permit laws after she and Sheri grabbed their quick bite today.

Sheri looked up from the broom she pushed around the shop and smiled. Today she wore a purple tunic shirt with black tights with matching eye make-up. Outlandish and just like Sheri. "It's usually me who's late."

Raleigh laughed. "I know. I got here as soon as I could."

Sheri waved a hand at her. "No big deal. Nick delivered our loaded fries from Danny's, and I got to spend a few minutes with him."

Raleigh sank into her usual stylist chair and gave it a twirl. "So, how is it going between you two?"

"Oh, you know," Sheri said, putting the broom away. "He says he's not sure what kind of commitment he wants, but then he acts like an old married couple. So, I'm not really sure anymore."

Raleigh nodded. "At least you two are together. I don't know what is going on between me and Mike."

"Nothing is going on between you two," Sheri said with a hand on her hip. "And nothing will continue going on with you two until one of you makes a move."

Grimacing, Raleigh stared at her reflection in the full-length mirror. "It's scary, though, to risk our friendship. I mean what if he has changed his mind?"

Sheri sank down onto the chair beside her. "Honey, he hasn't changed his mind. He's waiting for some signal from you that you are ready."

"But I told him I was, and then he said we needed to wait until the thing with Max had passed. Now it just feels like we are in limbo."

Sheri smiled, arching a heavily drawn in eyebrow. "The only way to get out of limbo is to tell him you are ready."

Raleigh shook her head. "He's in such a bad mood right now with his house and dealing with the insurance."

Sheri chuckled. "Well, maybe you can cheer him up with your charms."

Raleigh shook her head, frowning. "I'm serious. I don't know how to help him with this, aside from finding out who set the fire that is. That's really my only skill in the comfort department."

"You've been single for too long," Sheri said, fiddling with her bangs as she studied her own reflection.

"It's been a month," Raleigh said. "Lathan Babin wants a date with me, and Madison wants me to do her singles event, but I don't even know what my status is."

"Currently, your status is single," Sheri said. "It's up to you if you'd like to change it."

Raleigh could always count on Sheri's honesty. Now she needed to decide what she was going to do with the truth.

THIRTEEN

Raleigh shifted the cupcake box to her right so she could clearly see the pothole indented into the rough blacktop street. Maintenance on Cheramie Lane had grown lax along with every other small street in Barbeaux Bayou due to town funds being spent on levees to protect the lowlands from flooding. Years of neglect had taken its toll, and the streets crumbled.

Mike grumbled. "It's a good thing diabetes doesn't run in the family." An unusual frown played at the corners of his lip, and for the second time Raleigh thought about tossing the cupcakes at him.

The two had argued about the cans of beer in the brown paper bag he now clutched in his left arm. Paw would appreciate the beer, but Me'Maw chided Paw and his contributors when she spotted one in the old man's hand. Raleigh wasn't one to make the old lady unhappy, especially when they were in her home.

Raleigh bit her tongue and walked on. She didn't want to argue with grumpy Mike.

"The sugar will distract Me'Maw while you and Paw sneak off with that beer."

Mike walked alongside her and didn't respond. As they neared the front walk that would take them around back to the back door, Mike kicked his tennis shoe at the lump of St. Augustine grass growing through the cracked concrete. "I'm sorry I've been such a jerk."

Raleigh shrugged. "We're all given a pass once in a while."

He nodded and stared down at the pathway. Out back, the old chairs on the back porch were filled. A yip from an animal sounded as soon as they turned the corner, and Mike and Raleigh glanced at each other. Paw's dog, Spencer, had passed last month after sixteen years. He'd sworn no more dogs, but Raleigh had caught the old man looking toward the doggy bed on the back porch he hadn't had the heart yet to remove. Even though Paw was a quiet, unemotional man, she knew that the death of his daily companion had come as a blow.

Mason sat on the porch, his legs dangling over the side, and his arms clutching a chocolate lab puppy. The puppy's tail was beating Mason across the leg as it furiously squirmed to release itself from his grip. Mason's giggles echoed off the porch roof as he tried to wrangle the puppy in his lap.

"C'mon, Mom," Mason squealed. "It loves me."

From the old wooden porch chair, Madison shook her head, the set of her jaw saying it wasn't going to happen in this lifetime. "Maw said no animals, and we live with her. Sorry kid."

Madison looked anything but sorry. She looked as though she'd dodged a bullet, and she was thrilled to have an excuse to not be bringing home a puppy. Raleigh couldn't imagine Madison taking on the responsibilities of a puppy; she relied on a village to raise her son.

Lumbering over to Mason, Mike petted the puppy with one hand, still clutching his paper bag in the other. "Who does this little guy belong to?"

He looked around at everyone on the porch, waiting for a response.

Looking skeletal in her airy flowery dress, Amber tilted her head in her far away gaze. "My brother couldn't keep him in his new place with its no animals' policy, unfortunately. I thought Mr. Cheramie might want a new companion."

It took a moment for Raleigh to register that she was calling Paw Mr. Cheramie. Everyone called the man Paw, as he was everyone's Paw. Amber probably had her own Paw though, and some manners even with all her strangeness.

Paw shook his head, his five o'clock shadow catching the last rays of sunshine. "I'm too old to start training a new dog." He leaned forward in his old wooden chair and nodded his head toward Raleigh. "But Raleigh here could use a good guard dog as trouble seems to follow that girl."

Everyone chuckled, including Raleigh. Six months ago, a comment like that may have hurt her feelings, but now she took it as a form of endearment. Paw didn't mind the trouble she managed as long as she landed knee deep in it because she was helping people. What he didn't appreciate was drama caused by creating your own trouble.

Setting the box down on the porch boards, Mike coaxed the puppy from Mason's grip. The puppy whimpered as his long legs struggled to find a place, and then he curled up against Mike's chest. Mike looked at Raleigh and grinned at her, the first grin since the fire. He looked almost like the surfer, no worries guy she knew.

"A guard dog, huh?" Raleigh said, feeling a burst of warmth at his happiness. "Why not? I could probably use all the help I could get."

Mike chuckled as he snuggled the puppy to his chest.

She sure hoped Mike knew how to keep a puppy alive. She hadn't managed a plant thus far. That ivy in her kitchen was barely hanging on these days with its brown leaves outnumbering the green.

Later, after tucking the puppy away in a box placed between Mike and Mason's chair at the dining table, the group sat for a meal of shrimp and crab stew. The rich smell at the dining table lulled everyone into a silent stupor of clinking forks and dishes. With twice-a-week dinners at Me'Maw's, Raleigh could say good-bye to her size 6 jeans. With Madison's tiny figure, Raleigh didn't understand how the lithe girl could eat this heavy food every night between Me'Maw's and their mom's cooking, but watching her eat, though, Raleigh could see that she only picked at her food, barely eating. The creamy, medium colored roux with its mixture of spices was too good to just pick at and leave behind on the plate though.

Sipping from his beer bottle, Paw leaned back into his chair and looked around at everyone eating. Me'Maw had frowned when Mike had handed it to him, but she'd remained quiet in the new puppy excitement. The cupcake distraction had also helped.

Paw's eyes fell upon Raleigh and Mike at the end of the table. "Where are you two with that girl's murder down at Ol' Leroy's crawfish pond? Down at the gas station, Daniel said he's not doing too well right now."

Feeling as if she couldn't take another bite, Raleigh put her fork down. Paw was referring to the corner gas station by the bridge where his oldest friend from elementary school worked the front counter. Daniel's grandson owned the station now, so he didn't change tires or pump the gas anymore, but he greeted everyone and diagnosed the issues.

Raleigh said, "Emma had a bracelet in her pocket connected to another girl's murder from four years ago. The girls were the same age."

Mike nodded; fork poised in midair. "We were suspicious of the boyfriend, and it turns out he is the cousin of the first victim."

Paw lifted a toothpick in the air, one that Me'Maw would have placed at the table for him before the meal started. After fifty years of marriage, Me'Maw anticipated Paw's every need. "You two suspect this boyfriend?"

Mike and Raleigh exchanged a look. Neither of them wanted to believe that a student—another teenager—could be responsible for Emma's death. They'd worked with these students for a few weeks, and they wanted to believe that teenagers wouldn't be so horrible to each other. Even though Raleigh had taken the life of a fellow teenager when she was seventeen.

Mike shrugged. "I suppose we have doubts about it."

Paw nodded once and continued leaning back in his chair, thinking on it.

"Courtney Theriot, the girl from four years ago, had a secret boyfriend that no one was able to discover the identity of," Raleigh added.

"Oh," Amber said, looking up from the cards she'd been fiddling with between bites of food. "I remember her. Well, her sister Sarah anyway, and the two of us graduated together."

Mike set his fork down against an empty plate. "Really? What do you remember about her?"

"Not much." Amber shrugged. "She and I weren't that close in high school, but I do remember there being plenty of rumors circulating when it all happened."

Raleigh asked, "Anything about a boyfriend?"

"Well, it was probably just rumors," Amber said, "but there was a rumor that Courtney had something going with a teacher or a student teacher. It was all anyone would talk about, and a few brazen students attempted to question the teachers."

"Ugh," Madison said, her nose scrunched up in disgust. "Can you imagine crushing on old Mr. Boudreaux or getting it on with big bellied Mr. Henry? That sounds horrendous on so many levels."

Mike chuckled. "Both of those retired five years ago. The faculty at Barbeaux High is quite young now. There's at least ten teachers younger than Raleigh and I."

Paw grunted, his toothpick hanging over the edge of his lip. "I'd hope they're old enough to know better than to be involved with a student."

Raleigh tapped on the table thinking about how difficult it was to keep a secret between sisters, especially in high school when they shared a house. She and Madison had six years between them, and still she'd always been in her business. "Were Courtney and Sarah close?"

Amber smiled. "When we were kids, the two were very close.

They even hung out in the same group of friends. I think Courtney was only a year younger than Sarah. I was always jealous because my brother didn't care at all about what I was doing. Of course, he's eight years older than me and was out of college before I even made it to high school."

Mike looked at her, his eyes questioning. "What are you thinking?"

Raleigh glanced quickly at Madison, who studied her phone with an intense glare. "Maybe the sister knows more than she let on back then."

Paw nodded, his furrowed brow indicating his thinking. "Leroy's crawfish pond isn't easy to find either, so whoever this person is needs to have some kind of connection to Ol' Leroy."

Mike said, "Leroy's son Keith left the gate open that night. The question is was it a mistake or on purpose?"

Raleigh thought about that a moment. If Keith had left it open on purpose, then Keith had been at least in on it if not responsible. This would lead to a second teenager, and that didn't sound any better than one.

Raleigh said, "We need to start talking to these people."

Mike nodded.

"Raleigh," Madison said, "don't forget about Friday night. I've counted you among my number."

Raleigh froze, caught off-guard.

"Oh, and Mike," Madison said, her phone in her hand. "You should come, too. I need another eligible man on the list."

Mike's hand brushed against the sleeping puppy. "Where should I be going?"

"My singles' mixer at Lebasque's," Madison said with raised arched eyebrows. "Seven o'clock."

Mike glanced at Raleigh and then back toward the puppy. "Is Raleigh covering it for the paper?"

Raleigh felt the depth of the question resonating around the table.

Paw chuckled. "Of course, she is. Raleigh doesn't need to be going to one of Madison's shindigs now that you are in the house. I hear you moved some of my sister's things out of storage. There's an old album I'd like to see again."

Madison raised an eyebrow at Raleigh.

"I think that album is in the curio box," Raleigh said, ignoring Madison. "I'll look for it."

Mike continued petting the puppy and didn't bring it up again as the conversation turned toward the levee project that reached behind Paw's property.

FOURTEEN

Raleigh sketched an arrow on the side of her legal pad, pointing in the direction of the misshapen flower she'd penciled in earlier. Mike bumped his knee against her thigh, and she looked up at the table where Rachel from advertising's rambling had puttered out. For the last five minutes or so, the petite blonde had droned on about why no one wished to place ads in the print edition.

From behind his chair, David cleared his throat. He still clutched her rolled up one-pager in his hand as he looked at them across the table. "People will not like the size of their paper to change. The last time we tried that, I fielded complaints for months. I'd really prefer not to do that again."

Rachel jabbed a finger at the printout splayed across the table. "I can only sell what people will buy. Our television and radio ads are at an all time high with a 37 percent increase in sales. People aren't supporting print. What can I say?"

Raleigh jabbed her pencil into the top page, which is what she wanted to do to her eyes every time Rachel's nasally whine and big eyes widened to emphasize each word.

"We could begin to transition to Internet posting of news like every other newspaper." Raleigh's voice only hinted at her irritation.

David shook his head, tossing Rachel's report down onto the table. "Our community isn't ready for that kind of transition. Over half our audience probably don't turn on a computer in their day. We need a different solution."

Rachel stood and straightened her pencil skirt. "Well, let me know when you figure it out. Until then, I will try to solicit a few more sales."

The blonde grabbed her notes from the table and padded out in her three-inch heels.

Raleigh sighed. "She's quite annoying. I don't see how you can work so well with her."

David chuckled, as if Raleigh had made a joke and wasn't completely serious with the sentiment. "She grows on you after a while or maybe you just get used to her harshness. I don't know which is which, it's been so long."

Mike rested his arm against the back of the empty chair next to him. "Should we worry about the paper though?"

David twiddled with his eyeglasses, cleaning them against his cotton button down. "We are always worried, Mike, but this community likes their newspaper. I know this to be true because of the amount of complaints I field when Phillip forgets to toss one in a driveway."

Raleigh chewed on her bottom lip, thinking about future career plans if the newspaper folded. She didn't have much to offer in terms of resume skills. At least not any that would make her appear sane to future employers. Traiteur to the dead didn't make much sense to those outside of her small hometown.

Mike bumped against her leg again, interrupting her downward spiral of thoughts. "We just need to remind the community that the paper is important."

David nodded. "Right, right, right. And I want the same community stories that we always run. What do we have going on right now?"

Raleigh looked down at her notebook, ignoring the margin of doodles. "Council meeting to decide the fate of the dilapidated buildings in town, and the church's fundraiser for upcoming renovations."

"Don't forget about Madison's grand opening." Mike grinned. "I'm sure that will get the community talking."

"We'll decide if that's fit to publish after it happens." David frowned. "Where are we with the high school drowning victim? People will want an update."

Mike and Raleigh exchanged quick eye contact. "We are working on it," Raleigh said. "Chasing down leads as we speak."

"Good, good, good," David said. "Give me a mock-up of the layout when it's done."

"Got it," Mike said as the two of them stood to go.

"Raleigh," David said, then hesitated. "My niece is set to attend the opening event of Madison's new business. Should I be worried?"

Forcing down a smile, Raleigh cleared her throat. "No sir, everything is legitimate. I've been invited myself."

David nodded, his eyebrows still furrowed in concern. Raleigh didn't blame him. Madison hadn't built a reputation as someone whose party you wanted to send your innocent niece off to.

Raleigh followed Mike back to their cubicles in the fairly noisy floor. The TV production studio was preparing for several tapings today and everyone appeared to be in studio.

Sliding into his chair, Mike leaned back and looked at her. "So, you're going to Madison's mixer event?"

"No," Raleigh said, slapping her notepad down and touching her computer to make it come to life. "Madison is just being Madison."

Mike nodded before stirring his own computer.

"Someone will have to cover it for the paper..."

Raleigh typed in "Sarah Theriot" in her search bar. "You considering it?"

She tried to make her voice neutral, but her heart had cantered forward. If Mike attended, what did that mean? Was he sending her a message?

Mike shrugged. "I haven't really been in the mood to have fun, but I suppose we could cover it together."

Attending a singles' event with someone you wanted to date had to mean something. Raleigh wasn't sure if it was something good or bad. The not knowing could drive a person crazy.

She narrowed her eyes at her computer screen, trying to focus on something besides Mike's presence ten feet away.

After a moment of attempting to force the letters into focus, she clicked on "Sarah Theriot" and a host of listings from social media came through. The way this generation lived would make it impossible for a person to hide.

"Got her," Raleigh said. "She attends the parish's university. We could probably catch her between classes."

Mike nodded, grabbing his jacket from the chair. "Let's go. You can call her on the way."

Raleigh jotted a few key pieces of information down on her small notepad, and they headed out the door.

Thirty minutes later, the two sat at a small bistro table among a busy crowd in the common's area. When Raleigh had called, Sarah had offered to swing by during a break between two classes.

Mike looked around the milling students, seemingly not in a rush to get to class, to work, to home, to any particular spot. "Do you miss our college days?"

Sweeping across the tables near them, Raleigh took in a girl's nose nearly touching the pages of a thick book, and at another table, a young man napping with ear buds in and his head planted firmly on the table.

She grinned. "Only parts of it."

He chuckled. "You chose to get an English degree with all that studying."

Raleigh grimaced. "I don't know what I was thinking.

A petite strawberry blonde approached the table, a red cross body bag slung across her hip. "Raleigh Cheramie?"

Raleigh nodded, taking in the bare freckle face and ripped jeans. She looked twelve.

Flopping onto the chair, she dropped her bag next to the red plastic chair and slapped her hands onto the table. "We'll have to talk fast. Dr. V is the only professor I have that takes attendance, and of course, I have him next."

Raleigh sat up straighter, alert, feeling the pressure of a clock. "We were hoping to get some information about your sister."

She nodded, big deep bobs. "My mama told me you had stopped by the house. Look, I don't know what more I can tell you that I didn't tell those police when it happened."

Mike tilted his head in his easy going, you-can-trust me look that made the girls melt. "We are looking for details you may not have thought about earlier. Things that may not have seemed important back then."

Raleigh nodded. "Yes, like rumors that your sister was dating a teacher. You may have dismissed them back then, but what happened to trigger those rumors? It could be important."

"I see." Sarah chewed on her bottom lip and twisted the sleeve of a yellow plaid shirt.

An awkward silence grew as they waited, and she appeared deep in thought.

Finally, Raleigh leaned forward, looking in the eye. "Do you remember what was happening with your sister weeks before it happened?"

Sarah shrugged. "I can't say I paid much attention to her back then; I mean she was my little sister, you know? She was a pain, and at eighteen, I couldn't have been more self-centered."

Raleigh shook her head. "Trust me, I get that. I have a little sister, too."

"I guess I didn't ask enough questions." She sighed, a rugged raspy breath heaving though her heavy chest. "After much therapy, I forgave myself, but you always wonder what if you'd done things differently."

Raleigh shook her head again. "Little sisters always find a way to get in trouble. I think it comes with birth order."

She grinned. "I know." She shook her head, her hair ruffling around her. "She wasn't involved with an older man though. She couldn't be. That girl went to school, home, and to the home of the same friends she'd had since kindergarten. Once, she'd told me she had an older man interested in her, but I don't think anything came of it. She'd always been more daring than me and certainly more secretive, but not in a way that meant she would make a bad decision like that."

Mike's chair scraped against the floor as he moved closer to the table. "Do you know when or why the rumors about the teacher started?"

"Oh, probably a good six or so months before she died." Sarah swallowed. "At the time I thought it was because she was a teacher's pet and maybe one of those perverts had manipulated her into it. But Courtney had a perfect grade point average and was really smart." She shrugged. "I think kids were jealous and spread rumors after she received yet another award."

After working with the journalism class for only a few weeks, Raleigh could see that rumors started easily. "What about the bracelet? Did she ever give any indication about who it was from?"

"Ah, the mysterious boyfriend." Sarah's eyebrow rose. "I'm not sure if there was actually a boyfriend." She laughed.

"What do you mean?" Raleigh asked.

"When I fixed the clasp that day, she confided in me that she'd stolen it from her boyfriend." Sarah rolled her eyes. "Now who has to steal a gift from their boyfriend?"

"Any idea who she may have stolen it from?" Mike asked.

"A crush maybe?" Sarah shrugged. "Maybe you can ask her friends. Lindsey something or other was her best friend. She might know who she was crushing on."

A minute later she exited just as ceremoniously as she'd entered the student union.

"I don't know about you, but I have more questions now," Raleigh said as the two strolled back to Mike's Jeep.

Mike swung his arms back and forth. "I think we are getting closer to the right questions though."

Raleigh looked around as they passed young students going about. "What I wonder is what kind of person was Courtney Theriot. If she stole a bracelet, did she also stalk an older man? I'm wondering how much we really know about Emma and Courtney."

Mike nodded his head as they spotted the Jeep. "Yep. I'm thinking the same thing."

FIFTEEN

The odor emanating from the hanging herbs in various shades of drying caused Raleigh's nose to tingle. After sneezing three times in the last ten minutes, she'd tried shifting herself around the room, but herbs hung from cabinets and makeshift clothesline, and she couldn't escape the scent wreaking havoc on her sinuses. The overwhelming heat of Halona's workroom wasn't helping either, and a lack of ventilation only ratchetted the heat to sweltering.

Halona bristled back into the rustic workroom right off the kitchen. "Sorry about that. My son never understands my work. I suppose he's what we'd call Americanized."

Raleigh nodded. From their weekly sessions, she knew Halona spoke of her younger son, who had only five or so years on Raleigh. Halona's eldest son, Dardar, had trained extensively in her ways and had attempted treating Uncle Camille. Uncle Camille had taken to being an uncooperative patient, and Raleigh hadn't seen Dardar around in a few weeks.

Raleigh leaned back in an old metal chair. "What is Red doing these days?"

Halona shrugged as she fiddled with some jars on the counter.

"Suffering from a broken heart. He fell for a pretty blonde who fell for another pale skin fellow. He will learn one day."

Raleigh smiled. Bear, Red as they called him from a red feather he had worn around his neck for two years as a young boy to let everyone know he was Native American, had a thing for young pretty girls who didn't like him back. He'd made a habit of falling for the wrong woman and spent his time either chasing them or nursing a broken heart. Even though she'd only had two encounters with him at Halona's house, she felt as though she knew him from the old lady's stories and complaints.

Halona motioned toward the object on the old beat up worktable. "Let us return to our work."

Raleigh once again studied the carved wooden flute. Over time the wood had discolored in places and around several edges. The marks of a carving tool could still be found even with all the fingers that had worn it smooth in places. The flute was a crude, homemade instrument that Halona said had belonged to her own mother.

Raleigh hesitated in picking up the flute. "So, every object has this residual energy you speak of?"

Halona's chest heaved upward as she trailed a finger along her mother's flute. "The living leave behind an impression on the objects that they have spent their time with. The more love and energy they poured into the object, the more energy you will be able to absorb from the item. You must allow this energy, this impression of life, to enter you. Feel it in that space you speak of where the dying enters."

Halona was speaking about the hollow pit in her head that felt empty until the dead reached out and poured themselves into it. Since Cousin Joey needed her to use the ability to connect to objects for cold cases, Halona had decided that their next lesson should be focused on this. Raleigh was unsure of pursuing this. It felt like tempting fate—like chasing a ball into a sewer and expecting not to find a rat.

Raleigh ran a finger over the surface of the flute before picking it up. At first, she heard only a dog barking in the distance and Halona's heavy breathing. Slowly, a smoky blackness seeped in through the tips of her fingers, and headfirst, she pushed towards the edge of the blackness seeing a flickering light somewhere beyond. After pushing through the weight of water, she emerged to a dark night illuminated by a bonfire. The flames licked at the sky, a drum beating the rhythm of her heart. Then the melody of the flute began. Enchanting, slow, and calling to the ancestors of the clouds and stars to join them at the fire.

As she felt herself becoming one with the rhythmic dancing, Raleigh yanked back to the present.

Dropping the flute back onto the table, Raleigh recoiled from the beauty and hauntingness of it.

Halona's hands lingered on the table as she stared at her family heirloom. "I'm sure it felt different."

Raleigh felt the energy crawling along her flesh. "It wasn't like death, but it felt even stranger as if I was falling into it. I felt like I was plummeting, and I wouldn't be able to come out."

Halona's shoulders slumped. "When manipulating the forces of nature, there's always consequences."

As her eyes stared at the indentations in the flute, she thought about the dangers of this. "So, should I be doing this?"

Halona shrugged as her fingers stretched out toward her flutes. "Only you can answer that question."

Raleigh furrowed her forehead in concentration. She hated riddles, and Halona liked to speak in quaint idioms and folk proverbs.

Halona chuckled with her eyes closing to skips with her mirth. She knew that Raleigh didn't like this. "You have to decide if helping someone matters more than the consequences. That weight of that decision can only fall on you."

Raleigh felt the heaviness of obligation anchoring her to the chair. Acceptance of her "talent" had been a lifetime struggle, and for nearly a decade she'd shut the dying out. Only recently through her experience had she come to feel as if she owed those tragic lost spirits a resolution because only she could give it to them. She felt it to be true with all her being, but she didn't want to lose herself either. The idea of seeing loved one after loved one die caused enough fear. She didn't need this added burden.

Twenty minutes later after unsuccessful attempts at connecting to an old rag doll, Raleigh traveled the back roads of the Back Bayou trying to wipe the fuzzy feeling of being out of her head. Joey may have to accept a 50 percent success rate with those cold cases.

As she neared the dense trees of the street leading to the Back Bayou, Raleigh's cellphone rang. Braking at the dented stop sign, she reached over the console onto the passenger seat, realizing she'd emerged from the dead zone.

"Raleigh." Mike's voice echoed against emptiness. He must be outside. "Can you stop at the store and buy a different brand of puppy food? Luna doesn't like the one I bought."

Raleigh rolled her eyes as she looked both ways at the highway. "We are calling the dog Luna?"

"Just trying it out," Mike said sheepishly. "You don't like it?"

"It'll work." What would not work for Raleigh is all the howling the dog had done last night being stuck inside that box Mike had put her in to sleep. A name would have only provided something to yell out in frustration at 2:00 a.m.

"Okay," Mike said, a loud banging sounding in the distance, as if something hard had come in contact with wood. "There's a surprise for you when you get home, so don't forget the puppy food."

Hanging up, Raleigh considered the possibilities of what Mike considered a surprise. She hoped it had nothing to do with Luna, unless it involved getting the new puppy to sleep all night.

Pulling into the parking lot of the grocery story, Raleigh noticed a familiar sleek black sports car in the first parking slot. On a weekly basis, the car appeared down Cheramie Lane to whisk Mason away for a visitation. Raleigh preferred to mentally block Jeffery Zedeaux's connection to her family, but he continued appearing wherever she went as a reminder that he and Mason shared DNA.

Even though the grocery store wasn't some mega-conglomerate

chain store, she reasoned that she could get in and out without running into the man. Mrs. Liz Duet stood in the front bakery section sifting through the prebaked cakes as Raleigh entered. The old woman smiled and waved. Raleigh returned the greeting but feigned a hurry toward the aisles in search of puppy food—something she'd never purchased in her life. Must be a sign she was a grown-up—now if she could only get the lawn mower to start before the sixth crank.

On her way toward the upper numbered aisles, she glanced down the candy and potato chip aisle and caught Jeffery Zedeaux in jeans and a polo shirt, hands on hips staring at a section of flavored potato chips.

She passed quickly along although from her peripheral vision, she caught his glance her way. The two had happily avoided each other the last month as Madison had allowed him into Mason's life for the first time. Of course, Madison's motive involved avoiding a custody battle.

On aisle twelve, she grabbed a different color dog food bag than the one sitting by the back door at her house before hustling back the way she'd come. She didn't understand how the puppy could be picky as it all appeared the same on the bags, but she wanted to make this quick, so she wasn't going to consider the merits of the different ingredients today. She'd prefer to be anywhere Jefferey Zedeaux was not.

Before she reached the cashier's lit number three, Raleigh noticed that Jeffery still stood staring at the same section of chips. She'd never known the man to be indecisive with anything in his life. In fact, his inability to think beyond himself spurred him to take actions that Raleigh opposed on her own moral grounds. The two had faced more than one confrontation over his hasty actions.

Then the truth of his conundrum smacked her over the head like a container falling from Me'Maw's overstuffed cabinets.

She should continue walking and allow him to suffer. It would only be karma for all the people he'd caused suffering to in his life.

But dammit, she couldn't do it. She couldn't do it to Mason.

Turning around, she headed toward his aisle. Ignoring his glare, she reached beyond his tall form and grabbed a large bag of cheese puffs. Placing it in his hands, she turned and walked away, unable to disguise her smile. Mason loved the messy, no flavor snack. Raleigh kept them in her pantry for his visits and didn't complain too much when his orange fingers stained everything within his reach.

"Raleigh," Jeffery called, her name sticking in his throat.

Raleigh turned to face him, a suspicious and defensive glare already in place.

He swallowed, his throat bobbing at his effort to be civil to someone he detested. "Thank you."

With his curled lip and flat eyes, he looked as if he would have preferred to choke on the words than to let her think he meant them. He'd probably never imagined he'd say anything but insults to the one woman he'd been unable to seduce with his charms.

Nodding, Raleigh turned again and exited the aisle. That warmth in her belly may be pride—a feeling she didn't experience often. It wasn't enough for her to send Jeffery Zedeaux an invitation to family, but perhaps civil discourse instead of a brawl in a grocery store may be in their cards. Grabbing a bag of Twix at the end of the aisle, she told herself she deserved the celebratory reward. Anyone who knew the two of them would agree that a reward was in order. She could even share—but the pride hadn't made her feel that level of good.

Her overinflated pride carried her all the way home. As she pulled into her driveway, she could hear machinery grinding away in her backyard.

Mike's words on the phone about a surprise sent fear through her. Had her houseguest decided to make changes to her house in some way? Mike wouldn't do that, would he? The house remained a relic of her childhood, and she couldn't imagine his changes when she hadn't even moved the teapot yet.

Mike would have talked big changes over with her first though, wouldn't he? His moods had been spastic lately.

Turning the back corner of the house, Raleigh inhaled a nose and mouthful of fresh wood and sawdust particles. She coughed at the intrusion and her eyes watered.

The puppy barked as it ran toward her, but then it tripped over its own overly large paws. Amber laughed from her crossed-legged seat on the ground, where moments before she'd been playing with it as she gazed off in Mike's direction of the table saw.

Mike glanced up from the table saw and smiled. Raleigh had no idea where power tools had appeared from for this project, but the unfinished frame of a doghouse had taken shape under Mike's guidance.

Relief flooded through her. At least Mike hadn't started making changes to the house. Aunt Clarice could be a pretty angry ghost, and even as a ghost, the woman held power—the power to allow Raleigh to sleep.

"So, Luna's going to get a house outside?" Raleigh asked as the puppy nipped at her feet.

"One of us should have a house, right?" Mike shrugged as he shook his head of his thoughts. "I figured she could adjust to the house before she gets too big to run around the inside of the house."

"You could get another home again," Raleigh said, feeling the sulking that had come and settled in Mike's chest like a snuggled cat.

She's already agreed to the dog to cheer him up. An animal in the house felt like another incentive for Mike to pull himself out of this funk. Mike had his heart set on taking care of this dog inside her house. Well, even Paw had mellowed when he'd reached seventy. She'd have to figure this out.

SIXTEEN

With its peeling red stripes, the Down the Bayou Dinner hadn't held up well through its many years of servicing the young crowd. In fact, the building and the milkshakes and cheeseburgers hadn't been updated since Raleigh's parents dropped in after school in their early dating days. Time stood still in Barbeaux Bayou as the town and its businesses moved reluctantly into the twenty-first century with its few modern brick and mortar stores.

As Mike and Raleigh stepped onto the wooden decking wrapping around the restaurant, Raleigh said, "This place doesn't hold up to our memories, huh?"

Looking around, Mike shrugged. "I don't know. There's something to say about nostalgia."

Taking in the peeling paint and the rusty metal of the awning, she wasn't certain if memories could wipe out the here and now. "You think so?"

Mike grinned. "Do you remember all those baskets of fries Katherine would smother in mayonnaise? Who eats fries with mayonnaise?"

Laughing, Raleigh thought back to the days the three of them stopped in after last period and pooled their spare change together to share a large order of seasoned fries so covered in salt and cayenne pepper that your fingers burned between the hot grease and spice. The DB had been claimed by high school students since it had opened its doors and the age group that didn't care about blood pressure or health had occupied its seats.

"Yes, but the food's terrible," Raleigh protested. "Not the area's best representative of good bayou cooking."

Mike shook his head as his dimple showed. "My sister picks up burgers every Friday night for her and the kids. She claims they are great."

Raleigh scrunched up her nose in disgust. "Your sister still wears the same jeans she wore in high school, and the same hairstyle to match the acid wash. I think it's safe to say her taste hasn't changed."

Mike held the door open for her, peering inside over her head. "Yep, we're walking into a high school."

Walking inside, the smell of fried grease and burnt meat smacked her in the nose. The mismatched tables hadn't been updated, but it did look as though it had received a fresh coat of paint in the last decade. They'd thought coming to talk to Olivia and Keith on their turf might help get them to be more forthcoming. They'd discussed something about finding them in their natural habitat, but now as Raleigh looked around, she had to wonder what they were thinking.

No single individual over the age of eighteen existed in the diner except for an elderly cook, whose hair net stuck out from the cutout behind the counter. Even the two waitresses bopping around the mismatched chairs looked sixteen with their ponytails and fresh faces. Mike and Raleigh may as well have worn signs and bells announcing they'd come to chastise one of them and haul them home for bad behavior. At least that's how she felt when all of their eyes turned on the two of them blocking the exit.

Mike spotted Olivia in the corner first, and Raleigh trailed behind him as he weaved through the rowdy crowd. Raleigh looked to the left as a straw paper hit her, but no one looked their way as a familiar-looking student tossed a French fry across the table at a freckle-faced brunette.

Keith hadn't looked up from a basket of French fries until Raleigh bumped against his chair as another teenage boy jostled her from behind.

The lanky boy looked up, his curly, brown hair falling into his face. "Ms. C?" He shook his head, his eyes scanning the diner. "Not cool, just not cool, man."

Mike pulled out an empty chair from the table and flipped it around before sitting on it. "Give us a break. They weren't carding at the door."

He scrunched up his forehead as he stared blankly at Mike. "Huh?"

Raleigh laughed, feeling even older now. She slid in next to Olivia. "We wanted to talk to you about Emma, and we thought outside of school and your families might be the best place."

"Isn't there a law against that?" Olivia said, grimacing as she gave Keith a pointed look.

Mike swiped a fry from Keith's basket. "We're reporters, not police."

Raleigh leaned forward, closer to Olivia. The girl's green eyes and red hair made her a standout. Her makeup always looked airbrushed like a cosmetics advertisement, but every time Raleigh saw her, she wore a grimace on her lips.

Raleigh placed her hands on the table. "We were hoping you could tell us something about Emma that would help us figure out what happened to her. The two of you were best friends after all."

Olivia slunk back against the booth. "That doesn't mean I knew everything about her."

Mike fiddled with the napkin holder, avoiding looking at her. "Come on, you at least know who she's keeping company with?"

Keith shook his head, a look of pure distaste curling up his lips. "Keeping company with? Who talks like that, Mike?"

Mike pulled away from the napkin holder and sat up straight.

Anger flushed red through Mike's neck in splotches. Normally, Mike's temper was nonexistent, but since the house fire, Raleigh could see dark emotions brewing closely beneath his skin. He'd clammed up about it though. Maybe he'd confided in the puppy, but other than that hope, Raleigh would say he'd bottled it all up.

"Maybe you can help us out with something," Mike said, staring Keith down. "How would Emma or someone with Emma know about getting to your dad's crawfish ponds?"

Keith recoiled, his back slapping against the back of the plastic chair. "How am I supposed to know?"

"Seems fishy that your friend's body turns up in a place where you accidently left the gate open," Mike continued, staring him down.

"What are you saying, Man?" Keith said, his face darkening with his own anger.

Mike returned his glare.

"Come on guys," Raleigh said, feeling the tension raise her own body temperature. "Don't you want to know what happened to Emma? We are just trying to make sure someone answers for her death."

Tears sprung to Olivia's eyes, and she gazed down at her hamburger, twisting her hands in her lap. "I didn't think I'd miss her so much."

"Losing a friend is difficult," Raleigh said. "Mike and I lost our best friend in high school. We understand how you are feeling."

Olivia grumbled. "No one understands how I feel."

"I'm out," Keith said, standing. "The guys want me in the parking lot." He looked down at Olivia, his face softening. "I'll be back."

"Great, Keith," Olivia said sharply. "I can so depend on you to be here for me."

Keith's head bobbed. "I'm coming back, Olivia. Don't be dramatic about it. I'm needed outside."

Mike nodded. "Our conversation isn't done yet."

Keith sneered before slipping on a black hoodie and walking lankily toward the exit. Olivia rolled her eyes and huffed.

Mike slid into Keith's abandoned seat so that he now sat across from Olivia with direct access to her expressions. "What can you tell us about Emma before she died? What was going on with her?"

Olivia shrugged. "She'd gotten real weird."

Raleigh noticed how she wouldn't meet their eyes. In fact, she wouldn't lose focus on her hands in her lap. "Weird, how?"

Olivia shrugged again, her eyes roving around the dinner. "She'd become real controlling. Trying to tell everyone who to date and who to be friends with. It wasn't like her." Raleigh felt her leg bouncing up and down from the vibrating floorboards. "She and I had begun to drift apart because of it."

"But you were together that night at the bar," Mike prompted.

Olivia glanced up at him before snapping back to her fingers. "That was different. It was the whole group of us together. Until she and Jeremy left the group."

Raleigh looked to Mike and his eyes narrowed a bit. "Why did the two leave?"

Olivia sighed. "They were arguing, and Emma wanted to go home."

Mike tapped on the table, and she glanced at him. "Do you know what they argued about?"

Olivia grimaced. "He thought she was cheating on him. Jeremy could be very jealous, and Emma usually made sure he didn't need to be. But like I said, she'd been acting weird."

"And you saw the two leave to go home together?"

Raleigh waited, but Olivia hesitated. It was a brief pause, but it caused Raleigh to feel a surge of adrenaline that something else had been kept from them.

"Well, Keith did," Olivia said. "I'd already left."

Mike slouched back into the booth. "So, you left the group first?"

Olivia tilted her head sideways; all her red tresses covered the right side of her face. "If I would have missed my curfew, I would have been grounded for a week."

Raleigh was just about to ask her about Emma and Jeremy when the door flew open.

"Fight!" screeched a boy with dimples and a mess of curly hair before disappearing back outside, leaving the heavy metal door to slam shut in his wake.

Metal and plastic chairs scraped the wooden floorboards as the teenage clientele were drawn toward the violence like a magnet.

"Oh Lord," Olivia said, trying to push Raleigh out of the booth in her exit. "Keith is out there."

Mike jumped out the booth in one swift motion, and Raleigh followed as if on instinct. Joining the jostling crowd, Mike pushed through the center, and Raleigh attempted to follow before everyone spilled in behind him. Feeling a tug on the belt loop of her jeans, she realized that Olivia had latched onto her in order to move through the crowd quicker.

Outside, a crowd had gathered around a blur of two boys tussling. One boy had a scrawny arm around the neck of the other dust-covered boy, but the head-locked one swung his fist wildly at the face and head of the other boy—anything he could to make contact.

As they approached, Raleigh focused on the faces of the boys through the heads and shoulders of the teenagers gathered around gawking and cheering. The head-locked boy was Keith, and Jeremy had a firm grip on his neck that he wasn't releasing.

Mike lunged forward through the crowd and grappled with Jeremy to unlock his elbow and return blood flow back to Keith's face. On instinct, Raleigh dove in to help him. She clasped onto Keith's arm and yanked him in the opposite direction of Mike and Jeremy.

As a wild punch flew in her direction, she ducked, releasing her tug on Keith's elbow.

"Ms. C," a voice from her left side yelled out. "I got him."

Little Ray dove in and gripped Keith around the chest. A misnomer, "Little" had nothing to do with Little Ray's size, which was the size of an NFL tight end. The "Little" had been assigned only because his father was Big Ray, and Big Ray had at least a few inches and fifty pounds on his son.

Mike forced Jeremy's grip loose with sheer force, and Little Ray gripped Keith around his middle ten feet away from where he'd picked him up and carried him away from the tussle.

Raleigh's lungs tightened against the inhalation of gravel dust and old grease as she tried to regain her breath.

Olivia entered the fray, bringing her hands to her hip hugger skinny jeans. "What are you doing, Keith? This is crazy."

Keith struggled against Little Ray, who stood unwinded by the effort of keeping him contained. "Ask him," he spit out.

Jeremy kicked at the gravel of the parking area. "I can't help it if you can't handle the truth."

"Truth?" Keith gave up the struggle, glaring at Jeremy instead. "What truth? Your girlfriend is dead. You need to face it, and that's the truth."

Jeremy struggled against Mike as anger surged through him again, his face reddening with his pent-up fury.

"Easy now, boys," Mike said, his face red from the exertion of keeping Jeremy from lunging forward. "I'm sure we all want the truth here."

Jeremy elbowed Mike in the chest and freed himself as Mike flinched with the impact. "Forget it. People aren't interested in what I have to say."

Jeremy shrugged Mike away before elbowing his way through the crowd. Raleigh lost sight of him as he disappeared behind a navy pickup truck.

Little Ray released his arms from around Keith, who jerked around a bit kicking up gravel, trying to regain his pride, Raleigh supposed.

The crowd began to break up, herding itself back into the diner with a few stragglers gathering around a group of vehicles in the rear of the parking area.

Olivia pounced on Keith, her voice shrill. "What was that about?"

"Emma," Keith spit out, pumping his fist. "It's going to be about Emma until someone figures out what happened to her, right?"

He glared down at her, and Raleigh could see a level of angst and frustration that she'd probably only once known as a teenager, but Keith made her feel as if it were centuries ago.

Olivia stared at him, her brow furrowed, her lips squeezed tightly together.

Keith threw his arms up in the air. "I'm out of here."

Turning, Keith strolled toward an old beat up truck. He hopped in and peeled out in the rocks as he floored it.

Mike shook his head, his hair falling into place. "Don't worry. We'll go talk to him tomorrow."

Raleigh nodded, hoping that he'd calm down some in twenty-four hours. "Let's get through Madison's party first."

Little Ray shook his head as he approached. "Ms. C, don't you know better than to get in the middle of a fight? Those boys weren't worried about you."

Raleigh laughed. "I'm always in the middle of everything, it seems."

Olivia looked at her with a blank expression. "One day that's going to get you hurt."

SEVENTEEN

Raleigh's cellphone rang as she stood on the brick sidewalk contemplating her entrance into Lebasque's. A big wooden board sign announced Madison's shindig as "Heart's Entwined Get Together. Upstairs. 8:00-12:00." Raleigh would prefer to be snuggled up on her sofa doing a crossword puzzle than pacing outside the beautiful French-inspired building.

She reached for her cellphone and heard Joey's slow drawl on the other end.

"The bracelet may be a dead end."

Raleigh stepped aside and allowed a well-dressed couple to pass her on the sidewalk before entering the wooden arched French doors. This must be why Madison had come into her bedroom while she wasn't home today and laid out clothes on her bed for the evening with a sticky note that said, "Wear Me."

So not only was she going to a dating event, she was completely out of her comfort zone in heels.

She attempted to focus on Joey. "Why? What?"

A popping noise sounded across the phone. "Annabeth, I told you to be careful with that balloon." A muffled fumbling came over the line, and then Joey was back. "I brought the bracelet to the jewelry shop like you suggested, but they can't identify the owner because it is an antique."

"Could they tell you anything about it?" Raleigh asked as she paced across the red bricks. "Maybe where it was from?"

Another fumbling came over the line along with the high-pitched shout of a young girl. Annabeth must be fussing about the loss of her balloon.

"Henri at Bayou Jewelry said he'd guess it's about a hundred years old," Joey said. "Not bought in town or he would have record as his was the only jewelry store open that long ago."

Raleigh chewed her bottom lip but tasted the bitter taste of lipstick and stopped. "What about the engraving? Was he able to tell you anything about the carving or the words?"

Joey coughed. "He thinks the engraving is newer based on the shapes of the letters. He gave me a few people to try to see if I get lucky on that end. So far, I got nothing."

Raleigh thought about the numerous possibilities outside of Barbeaux Bayou if the bracelet had originated beyond their small town, which it had, in all likelihood. Most people did their shopping outside of town to have more options available anyway. But one hundred years ago people didn't travel to shop. It was more likely that the bracelet traveled here with someone.

This revelation would not make it easier to track down the bracelet's owner or how it had come to be in the possession of two dead girls at some point during their lives.

"So, in other words," Raleigh said, "we'd need to rely on a person coming forth and saying they recognize the bracelet and knew something about who it belonged to."

Joey grunted. "That's about what I got right now."

"Can you get me a picture of the bracelet?" Raleigh said, considering what they had heard so far from everyone. "Perhaps we can ask as we talk to people."

"Sure thing," Joey said. "Now let me get back to Annabeth. She'd done gone and tied a balloon to the cat. Don't know why Sue Ann bought that girl a dozen balloons."

Raleigh laughed as they hung up. Annabeth sounded like a girl she would have been friends with at four years old.

Turning to face the gas lamps flickering on each side of the arched antique wooden, beveled glass door, Raleigh braced herself for entrance. If Mike hadn't have had to go to his mama's rescue and fix a clogged sink, she wouldn't be walking into this sure-to-be-a-disaster date alone.

As she lugged open the heavy door, a hand reached above her and pushed it easily open. "I see we are both attending the town's premier event," Lathan Babin said, looking down at her, his sport coat open wide from his exertion.

Raleigh stepped through the door to ease the uncomfortable nearness between them. "More like roped into what I hope isn't a disaster."

Lathan chuckled. "Come on, it won't be that bad. Food, drinks, and attractive people. What more could you ask for?"

Raleigh smiled politely, thinking about maybe a Twix bar, her pajamas, a sofa, a good book, and any number of antisocial elements the night could provide.

The two were halfway up the stairs to the second-floor event without another word when he turned to her again. "Were you able to find out anything more about Emma?"

Raleigh shook her head. "We're working on it, but we have come up against a bunch of dead ends. We think students know something, and we will get to it, we hope."

Lathan frowned. "That's so sad. Maybe something will turn up."

They reached the top of the stairs, and a young blonde waved at him and he walked off without another word.

Raleigh spotted Madison flitting around the room introducing people as the dashing handsome Federico Taylor followed her around like a doting Labrador retriever. It was such an unusual sight that Raleigh had to stand still and watch as it happened. With his reputation, he was known for attracting the young blondes, not being the lapdog of the poor brunette. And there were plenty of pretty blondes floating around the room.

As she scanned the room for familiar faces, she noticed Winter lifting a tray of glasses around the milling small groups. From the bubbling overflow of champagne, Raleigh would assume that Madison hoped to loosen up the vibe and celebrate at the unofficial soft launch of her business.

Raleigh crossed the crowd until she could be in the blonde-bobbed haired beauty's trajectory and waited.

Winter grinned, her blue eyes ice cold under the bronze eyeshadow. "Didn't imagine seeing you among the desperate."

Raleigh rolled her eyes. "Madison said I had to come as a favor. She's always calling for favors but never gives any."

Winter laughed. "I can see that. I'd rather be the cocktail waitress than mingle with this crowd of vultures."

"I thought you were working at the Seafood Camp bar," Raleigh said.

"Oh, I am," Winter said, her eyes roaming the room as she adjusted her tray, "but Lebasque gives me three days a week. Typically, it involves kitchen prep." She winked.

Raleigh felt as if there was something she'd missed in context. She looked away at the growing crowd. Mike still hadn't arrived, and the room had become a who's who of Barbeaux Bayou. Every eligible single must have received an invitation, and they'd all turned up. Even Max, former boyfriend, stood off in the corner sipping from a champagne flute as he spoke to three individuals, two male and one female.

Winter dipped in close. "Let me introduce you to Antoine. He's safe."

Raleigh nodded, thinking she could use a distraction until Mike arrived.

Antoine stood alone propped up against a column, sipping champagne as he studied the crowd. His acorn eyes flickered as they

approached and looked her over as Winter made formal intro-
ductions.

"I'll leave you two." Winter winked. "I need to get to our new
arrivals."

"So, what do you do?" Raleigh asked, feeling the uncomfortable-
ness as Winter walked away.

"Ah," Antoine grinned, his long chestnut hair ruffling against the
open collar of his shirt. "I do accounting for Federico."

Raleigh laughed, unable to prevent it from escaping. "I'm sorry.
You don't look like any accountant I've ever met. I thought you were
going to tell me something outdoors like charter fisherman."

She realized how awful that sounded to a stranger as soon as the
words escaped, but she couldn't seem to stop them from tumbling
out.

He chuckled. "I do spend quite a bit of my time on a boat. Fishing, snorkeling, and anything really. I love the water."

"I apologize if I overstepped," Raleigh said, feeling her cheeks
burn. "I work for the Barbeaux Gazette, so questions are kind of my
specialty."

He nodded. "Winter has told me before about what you do."

Raleigh puzzled over his words only a moment before she realized the subtle meaning. "So how long have you and Winter been
dating?"

He shook his head and then leaned in. "Did you know that
through your special way?"

Raleigh laughed. "No, I'm just observant."

Well, at least most of the time. Sometimes she felt like her head
was in the water and her thoughts were churning slowly.

Antoine looked around. "We haven't really announced it yet, so if
you don't mind..."

Raleigh nodded. Winter must have introduced Raleigh as a cover.
The wild child must have her reasons, but Raleigh's sister left her
enough drama to deal with; she didn't need two divas to take care of.

It turned out that Antoine had moved here only three months ago after he'd been hired to figure out why money had disappeared from Federico Taylor's accounts. He wouldn't provide the details, but Raleigh gathered that Federico trusted the man due to childhood experiences in a boarding school. Even though Raleigh's curiosity was piqued, the volume of the room reached proportions where a private conversation could not be had.

When they parted, Raleigh realized that Mike had arrived, but he and Nate were speaking to two bottle blondes near an hors d'oeuvre table. One of them looked like Ginger Sappleton, who had been a quiet cheerleader in high school.

Instead of disturbing the group, Raleigh sought out Madison, who was dealing with a young girl in the corner near the staircase.

"But I was invited..." the girl said, trailing off into a whine.

Madison's crossed arms didn't budge, and neither did her raised eyebrows. "I'm sorry, but you must be 21 to attend this party. You will have to message whomever invited you that you cannot enter."

The girl huffed, stomping a five-inch heel down onto the wooden floor. "That's not fair. I'm not asking to drink."

The blonde with tresses down the middle of her back looked familiar, but Raleigh couldn't place her. They definitely hadn't attended high school together because clearly from her fresh face the girl hadn't even thought about twenty yet.

"Ugh!" The girl stomped her foot once again before turning and stomping loudly down the staircase. Clearly, she possessed the maturity to attend an adult party.

Madison gave Raleigh a grimace of frustration. "That's the second nineteen-year-old I have had to make leave tonight. I wish I knew who'd invited them, so I could ask them to leave as well."

"Other than that," Raleigh said, turning to face the room, "it seems to be going well."

Madison nodded. "Everyone's mingling. Do you want me to introduce you to Federico?" She raised her eyebrow and shook her head. "Maybe he'll be attracted to you instead."

"Problems already?" Raleigh asked, trying not to smile.

"Clingy," Madison said. "Who would have thought?"

Raleigh had to agree. His reputation had him as noncommittal, not a lovesick puppy.

"I think I'm going to head out," Raleigh said as she watched Mike and Nate tell a story.

Madison groaned. "Already? You will be single forever with your attitude. You and Antoine seemed to be having a good vibe."

Raleigh laughed. "I think he's interested in someone."

Madison waved her hand. "He's a playboy, just as must as your boy Lathan Babin."

Raleigh searched the crowd and found Lathan rather close to the two women from earlier. She wondered if Madison had checked their IDs because they didn't look much for the drinking age either. Lathan had been interested in her attending some school function with him, but he didn't seem interested at all tonight. Nor did she appear to be his type.

"Still," Raleigh said. "I'd prefer to figure out who I want to date in a more solitary environment."

Madison leaned in. "I don't blame you. That's why tonight I had an idea, but I'll share it later after I work out the details."

Since she stood near the stairs, Raleigh decided not to disturb anyone as she left. Mike seemed enthralled in his conversation, so she decided to let him be. He'd always been one to be interested in women for a short time—they'd once nicknamed him three-date Mike. Watching him engage in conversation was reminiscent of how all those dates had begun. And that nagging voice in her head that told her that a relationship could potentially be a bad idea yelled louder as she watched them laugh together.

Downstairs, she nearly ran into Max as he swung the door open.

"Excuse me," he said. She caught the moment it registered in his eyes that it was her. "Oh, I'm sorry, Raleigh. Leaving so soon?"

Raleigh smiled, a forced upturn of her lips. "I showed up as a favor, and now my part is done."

Max nodded. "You know if Madison Cheramie throws a party,

the Barbeaux police have to be there. It just so happens I'm one of the few single detectives."

Raleigh nodded stiffly, silently cursing the sheriff. Madison hadn't done anything illegal in at least six months, and even before that Breaux couldn't make anything stick.

"Well, good night," Max said.

"Night," Raleigh said, turning back toward the door.

Raleigh wondered if he'd gone to call it in to tell them it was a normal party. It infuriated her. She didn't even know why. Typically, she wished for karma to play fair with Madison, but she didn't want the sheriff to be karma.

Time to have a conversation with Sue Ann. Joey needed to oppose that man in the election. He just had to do it.

EIGHTEEN

Raleigh placed the water bottle in front of Sue Ann and then leaned back against the kitchen sink, crossing one leather boot over the other.

Sue Ann picked it up and fiddled with it without opening it. "So, you really believe Joey should run for Sheriff?"

Nodding, Raleigh said, "Joey is the most respectable man I know besides Paw. The family connections will help, not to mention everyone knows Joey is an honest, hard-working man."

Sue Ann smiled, pride shining her cheeks. "He's such a good man. Annabeth gives him a run for his money though." Sue Ann twisted the top of the bottle. "Both of us actually. Joey says she inherited the wild woman streak of the Cheramie women."

"Lord help us all," Raleigh said, grinning. "But at least you know she'll be able to take care of herself one day."

Sue Ann nodded, laughing. "You all seem to do that well. So, I am guessing you want me to talk my husband into running."

Raleigh smiled sheepishly. "I've mentioned it to him, and he said he would talk to you. I didn't want him to doubt himself and let the opportunity pass him by."

Sue Ann tapped the bottle on the counter. "Slow and meticulous with his decisions. That's my husband."

"And maybe he needs a push in the right direction." Raleigh raised her eyebrows.

Sue Ann looked at her a moment and then slowly nodded. "You Cheramies sometimes need a push."

Raleigh gave her a look of puzzlement.

"Joey tells me you are having trouble with the cold cases."

Staring down at her boots, Raleigh thought about her lack of reliability with objects. Guilt burned her esophagus every time she dwelled on it.

Sue Ann tapped her fingers on the counter. "I'm sure you will figure it out."

Raleigh opened her mouth to reply when Luna, the puppy, tapped down the hall. She'd traveled back and forth several times between the kitchen and front sitting room where Sheri, Mike, and Madison waited for her to plan the anniversary party.

"I'd say that's my cue to get going," Sue Ann said, sliding off the barstool. "Annabeth will have driven my mama crazy enough for one day."

"Thank you for coming by and listening to me though," Raleigh said, reaching down and rubbing Luna's head as she pushed her nose against her jeans.

"No problem," Sue Ann said, "I appreciate any time I get to leave the house for errands." She laughed.

Raleigh walked her to the door. Luna ran into the living room as Sue Ann waved to the lounging party and took her exit.

Raleigh sauntered into the living room and took her place on the end of the sofa.

Mike eyed her. "Did she get on board the Joey-for-Sheriff Express?"

"I think so." Raleigh nodded. "She agreed to talk to him. We have to get a new sheriff one way or another."

Mike chuckled. "Next thing I know, you'll be running."

Sheri twisted her head with attitude. "Barbeaux Bayou will freeze over the day that Raleigh Cheramie gets on that side of the law."

"Hey," Raleigh said, feigning hurt, "never underestimate me."

Sheri laughed a big, chest-deep laugh.

Luna scratched at the coffee table where the coffee cups and cookies lay scattered about in a haphazard arrangement. Her whimpering drew another chuckle from Sheri who lay lounged in Aunt Clarice's corner chair.

"You know, pets are just like kids," she said, waving a chocolate chip cookie in the air.

From her armchair, Madison reached for her coffee cup. "Which is why Mason doesn't have a dog. He can come play with Nanan's anytime."

Mike scooped up Luna and snuggled her against his chest. The puppy struggled a moment before burying her face in Mike's polo shirt. "She's a great companion, but she's just a puppy."

Sheri laughed. "You mean a bundle of energy that chews up shoes? NO different than a toddler. I remember Shawn chewing on everything he could put in his mouth. Child proofing, my behind. You'd have to leave just four walls in a house, and then they'd probably chew on the walls."

Madison's brow furrowed. "I was so glad when Mason outgrew that stage. It's hard to fathom having another baby now that he's older."

"Is that a possibility?" Alarmed, her hands suddenly needed to move so Raleigh straightened out the party planning sheets Madison had brought with her for Me'Maw and Paw's anniversary party.

Shaking her head vigorously, Madison said, "I'd have to be in a relationship to even make that possible."

Sheri tapped her sandaled foot in the air. "So how is it that our match maker has not found love?"

Madison shook her head. "Love is complicated, and I'm currently allergic to complicated."

Raleigh raised her eyebrows. "Complicated appears to involve two of Barbeaux's royalty following you around."

Madison rolled her eyes. "Ugh. Don't remind me."

Sheri huffed. "How do you manage? You must possess some charms we don't get to see."

Madison glared at Sheri.

"I noticed Jeffery Zedeaux wasn't there last night," Raleigh said quickly.

"I thought it was a bad idea," Madison said sharply, then she sighed. "Jeffery would like me to give him another try, but I'm just not sure."

The puppy whimpered as Mike shifted positions on his side of the sofa, and he rubbed her head in comfort. "I'm not the biggest fan of the man's, but he does seem to have a thing for you. Must be something with the Cheramie blood since he dislikes your sister as much as he likes you."

"Thanks," Raleigh said. "I'm just not most men's type."

Madison grinned. "Antoine seemed to be your type."

Raleigh laughed, her cheeks burning. "He was bored. He's covering up that he's dating a certain someone. Probably doesn't want to ruin his reputation just yet—or hers."

"Oh," Sheri said, her voice rising. "Scandalous. Almost as interesting as Madison having the two most eligible bachelors of Barbeaux chasing her."

"Aren't we supposed to be planning a party?" Madison asked frustrated. "Not dissecting my nonexistent love life."

Sheri chuckled. "Get used to it, honey. We like to balance the ever-present dead vibe with a little love around here."

Madison attempted a frown, but a laugh burst forth instead as she looked at the three of them. "I'm so lucky to have only inherited the good looks and intelligence from the Cheramies and not the freaky talents."

"What?" Raleigh said in mock defense. "You're training to be a traiteur. I wouldn't say that's high on the normal scale."

Madison waved her pages wildly in the air. "I plan parties. Run a business. You can keep the family vocation. Besides, Uncle Camille only rambles now. He wanders and rambles, so it's unlikely the family business is continuing."

Their uncle had taken up long walks that required someone to pick him up wherever he ended up and then he would sleep for two days. Uncle Camille was ill, and his days of doing anything with the living were numbered. The family didn't speak about this impending reality, not even in whispers. It was denial at its worse.

From Mike's lap, the puppy's head bounced up, and it leapt toward Raleigh's lap. She and Mike sat on either end of the sofa with a blue pillow between them. He'd returned two hours after her last night, and nothing had been said between them. It seemed to sit on the cushion between them though as they didn't mention the fact that their friendship of 25 years could continue as is or they could face the possibility of dating.

Madison frowned at the puppy. "Did anyone look over the party ideas yet? Isn't that our purpose today anyway? I do have launch party details to finalize for tonight."

Sheri flipped through the pages in her hands and raised a heavily black-lined eye. "Why exactly are we having seven musicians?"

Madison rolled her eyes as she slapped her hands against her knees. "It's Paw's favorite swamp pop band. Trust me, I would certainly scale back if my dad wouldn't want to do that for him. Everyone has offered their two cents on what this party should have."

Petting the puppy's head, Raleigh listened as the two debated the merits of swamp pop's music commerciality. Mike fiddled with his cellphone and paid no attention to the conversation. Trying to focus on anniversary gift ideas for her grandparents, she avoided looking at Mike's phone. She wondered if he had plans with the blonde from last night. Should he tell her this? Was that the level of their relationship now? Particles floated in the air, and Madison and Sheri swayed gently before her, so gentle that she almost missed the movement.

With her hand, Raleigh reached out and swiped at the air. Was that dust? She'd cleaned last week because Paw would comment if she didn't.

Mike looked up from his phone and looked at her. "Ree?"

Raleigh looked into Mike's concerned green eyes, and they blurred a muddy hazel.

Realization sank through her like an anchor in water as blackness overtook her.

Blinking rapidly against the darkness, murky cloudiness grew where blackness had existed only moments before. Slowly, small particles began to take shape before her, and she hoped her eyes weren't just playing tricks on her as the darkness caused panic to rise.

She strained to focus and produce something from nothing; a string of dancing seaweed brushed against her face and appeared to her. She wanted to reach and brush it away, but her hands wouldn't respond to the signals her brain was sending. She stared at her fingers, strange tentacles floating in the water.

She felt the water creep inside her as it suspended her in a cocoon. It began to burn.

Then a hand grabbed hers.

Keith's face extended from the top of the hand.

In fright, she yanked her hand away, but he tugged hard to keep his hold.

Panic tightened in her throat. This wasn't the way of things.

His eyes stared into hers as he squeezed her hand. And then his last moments pulsed through her palm.

He'd been disoriented. The sky was topsy-turvy. His feet stubbed against the oyster shells. His mud boat had been here only moments ago where he'd tied it to the dock to run back and grab his cap.

If it were here, he could fall into it and catch himself.

The water stung as he face-planted against the surface. His hands and feet wouldn't cooperate as he struggled with the water swallowing him. The burning began in the back of his throat—the painful fire of no oxygen.

How could Olivia betray him like this? He'd never get to tell her that he knew it all.

Pain spurned through him as his consciousness waned.

Raleigh panicked as she watched him drown.

Or he'd already drowned, and she was only now seeing it.

She wasn't returning to her own body.

Raleigh struggled against the grip of their clasped fingers, but he wouldn't budge even as his body convulsed.

Squeezing her eyes shut, Raleigh willed herself back into her body.

Mike's voice tunneled through the blackness behind her eyelids. "Raleigh? Do you hear me?"

Trembling, she opened her eyes to her own living room, staring up at the white, clapboard ceilings.

"I hate water," Raleigh grumbled, feeling the firm boards beneath her aching backside. She'd slid off the sofa during her struggle to return to her body.

Mike offered her a hand to help her up from the floor. "Where are we headed?"

Raleigh gave him one hand and rubbed her backside with the other. "The boat launch."

She could not bring herself to say that Keith, another teenager from the journalism class, had drowned.

She hoped this time she was wrong.

NINETEEN

Mike ended his call and tossed his cell phone on the dashboard of the Jeep. Tapping his fingers on the steering wheel, he stared out the front windshield.

"Joey has Buddy meeting us down at the boat launch," Mike said, signaling a left turn at the bridge. "He's going to tell the sheriff after the fact."

Raleigh nodded, hugging her arms tightly across her chest. She couldn't shake the tremors ravaging her body since emerging from the water. The connections she self-corrected. In the past it would end when the boy would be pulled from the water. She hoped this time it would be the same, so she could return to normal concerns like if Joey's career would suffer because of her.

Fidgeting with the shift, Mike glanced in Raleigh's direction and then reconnected with the empty road.

Raleigh felt the space growing between them as more and more went unsaid between them. "What?"

Mike shrugged as his lips twisted in agitation. "Are you sure?"

Glancing at her, his expression changed to acceptance as she glared at him.

Shaking his head, he shrugged. "I know that you're right, but I don't want you to be, you know what I mean? That's the second kid."

Raleigh nodded, looking out the passenger window at the gas station and its stack of tires along the chain link fence. Mike's face had frozen in shock when she'd told him who was in the water. The necessity of getting to Keith had propelled them forward, but he'd been unable to comment.

As they turned onto the old iron bridge, Raleigh said, "Do you ever regret being involved in all of this? I mean, do you ever think, I wish I could wipe all of this death from my life?"

Mike frowned, accelerating to make the green light. "It's not that simple."

As they passed the rolling lawns with cypress trees and hanging moss, Raleigh rubbed the scar on her wrist. "It could be."

Mike swung the Jeep at a sharp right turn into the boat launch gravel, the tires grinding to a halt near an aluminum boat trailer attached to a cobalt blue pick-up truck. "Death will always happen. If I remove myself, it doesn't mean that these people will still be alive. All I would do is stop helping, and I don't want to be that person that just hears about someone's death and doesn't do anything to help them find justice or peace, whichever is necessary."

Raleigh continued to stare out the window, tears burning her eyelids. Dammit she wasn't going to cry.

At four years old, when Mike had offered her that mud pie, fate had known what it was doing. Now if fate could only give her a sign now or interfere somehow and show them what to do.

Joey's patrol car rolled to a stop next to the Jeep, and he adjusted his cap as he stepped out. Raleigh and Mike met him at the bumper.

Joey looked around, and Raleigh followed, taking in the serene stillness of the tree leaves and the weeds sashaying in the gentle breeze. Joey said, "Beautiful scene for violence."

This boat launch had been her cousin Claudia's last resting place as well. At least Claudia had survived her wild ways until her mid-twenties whereas Keith had only been sixteen or seventeen. She had to agree with Mike on this one—dead kids were too much.

The three approached the waterline where the water lapped gently against the coarse cement runners into the canal. A deserted mud boat floated twenty feet from shore giving the only sign that something might be awry.

When foreigners pictured the swamps of Louisiana, places like the canal before her were the images of the photographs. People couldn't see the stench of stagnant water or the overgrowth of grass, but beyond that, even locals had to get off the beaten path for these scenes anymore. Most of the cypress trees were being cut down to pave the way for subdivisions and a new golf course.

Raleigh loved the view—from afar. Water left her leery of the depths and terrors hidden beneath the surface. Her throat constricted, and she struggled to breathe. She always felt as though the muddy water would swallow her.

Joey walked closer, the water lapping over the toes of his boots. Gazing deep, he stooped down and looked at something hazy beneath the surface.

Raleigh approached, attempting to peer at in the oyster shells and see what he'd noticed. She could never see what these men saw.

Joey looked up at her, the corner of his eyes wrinkled. "There's blood."

A dull thump in her cranium reminded her that Keith waited for her below. She closed her eyes, she saw the dim light from beneath a layer of water, and she knew he wasn't far out from the shoreline. If she knew a direction, she could probably walk out and brush against him—not that she was going anywhere near the murky water.

Mike squeezed her shoulder.

Joey stood and walked the edge of the water, pointing as he went. "Blood trail along the water's edge," he mumbled.

Taking his cap off, he scratched his head with the same hand. "I'm calling it in. I'll deal with the sheriff after."

Raleigh knew that Sheriff Breaux had placed a ban on following any tips from her. She was essentially *persona non grata* to the Barbeaux Sheriff's Office. Going against his boss could be career suicide for Joey, and she appreciated it at the same time that she hoped it wasn't foolish. Too much pressure on her to get it right. Not that she seemed to get it wrong, even when she wanted to.

Forty-five minutes later, Mike and Raleigh paced behind the yellow crime scene tape, anxiously waiting for Buddy to signal that the body was ready to be brought up. They'd painfully watched him plow around in the water in hip boots, poking around for a body with a long stick. Keith's anticipation bubbled in her head and caused her equilibrium to be off-balance.

Raleigh kicked at a rock and bit down on her lip, trying to calm down. Max's navy Caprice arrived on scene, and an officer lowered the tape to allow him through. In his stroll across the shells, he did not glance in Raleigh and Mike's direction. At the water's edge, he conferred with Joey before walking the shells and performing his own sweep. As Raleigh watched the scene unfold, a few more squad cars pulled up blocking the Jeep in further.

Mike leaned against the Jeep. "Sue Ann is going to be upset with us if we get him fired."

Raleigh rubbed her scar, feeling the motion offer some calmness. "Maybe we should buy her a gift basket with those lavender bath soaps she loves."

The two exchanged looks and laughed, a short-lived chuckle as they remembered the tragedy of the location. It did serve to relieve some of the tension growing as they waited.

Finally, Buddy gave a quick jab of his thumb, and gears screeched to life. Within seconds Keith's body emerged, water cascading back into the canal from the makeshift gurney cocooning his remains.

Pacing the shoreline, Joey waited for the gurney to reel Keith's corpse in front of him so he could inspect it. After only a moment, he swore, swiping his cap off. He glanced back at Raleigh and then hung his head before getting back to his study. Max joined him, his face devoid of emotion.

From their distance, Raleigh could only clearly see the water leaking down, turning the white shells gray.

Mike swore, crossing his hands over his chest. "We just saw him."

She nodded. Joey walked their way, his head deeply bowed. "We need to figure out what is going on before we lose another one."

Mike grunted. "Teenagers dying. Houses burning down. Something big is going on."

Joey came to a stop near them, a frown tugging hard at the corner of his lips. "It's Ol' Leroy's son. I hate to have to tell that man that he lost his only son."

"Poor man." Mike shook his head. "His crawfish pond is still closed and now his son is gone. Leroy will need help to survive this."

Joey grimaced. "Worse is that his head was bashed in, so it's going to be an intrusive investigation."

Raleigh looked back over the water, trying to avoid the clean-up scene with the coroner right now. Keith had stumbled around in shallow water. If someone had been here, he would have been alive. She knew this although autopsy and forensics would have to prove it. "His last thoughts were disbelief that his girlfriend had betrayed him."

Joey and Mike both looked at her with puzzled expression, and she shrugged. "His thoughts weren't that she'd done it, but that she'd betrayed him."

Raleigh hated to think that Olivia could be responsible for something so horrendous. Something had happened to Keith and Emma, and Raleigh would prefer if the someone who'd done it were someone they didn't know.

Mike ran his fingers through his hair. "Keith also argued with Jeremy yesterday at the diner."

Joey nodded. "Interesting that he keeps popping up in all the wrong places, but we can't seem to pin him down for questioning."

Raleigh looked to Mike. "I think it's time we get serious about getting the truth from these teenagers."

Mike nodded and Joey hmphed.

They needed to start with Jeremy. The boy needed to give up what he knew before someone else ended up dead in the water.

TWENTY

Scrunching up her nose at the odor of rotting fish guts and stagnant water, Raleigh took a breath through her mouth and held it instinctively. The docks were only twenty feet from the marina's tackle shop, and boats coming in from Gulf fishing trips offloaded their ice chests and debris freely. The sunshine wasn't doing the decaying carcasses any favors in the smell department, and the breeze carried just enough to cover the area with festering odor.

Mike lifted his sunglasses and scanned the boats coming in beyond the docks. "Boats are coming in for the day. Let's see if we can catch her before she gets too busy."

Raleigh could see a woman in blue jean shorts and a black apron shoveling ice from a large freezer into ice chests as two red-faced men gestured and told a boisterous story.

Peering closely, Raleigh tried to find a resemblance between this woman and Jeremy. Maybe the hair color? That dusty auburn. Ms. Dana's face appeared weathered, the wrinkles folded upon themselves and sunspots splattered throughout her face, neck, chest, and arms. Where Jeremy was tall and lanky, she was short and stocky.

As Jeremy's mom moved around her work area, Raleigh could

categorize few similarities, including their walk or stance. Jeremy must have taken after his father.

As Mike and Raleigh approached, Dana glanced up while continuing to scoop the ice. "I'll be with you in a moment, but you need a receipt from inside before I can load you up."

Mike stepped forward and aided her by holding up the lid as she worked. "We're actually here about Jeremy."

Raleigh stepped closer, shutting the gentleman involved in the telling of the hardest fish to reel in today out of view. "We're concerned about what has been going on with him."

Dana paused mid-scoop, several pieces of ice shattering against the cement. "Who are you again?"

"We work at the school with the journalism class." Raleigh smiled, hoping to appear friendly and not like a child predator. "Have you seen your son recently?"

The woman huffed, continuing with her ice. "As a matter of fact, I haven't seen him in two days. The boy says he needs his space. A teenage boy thing, I guess."

Raleigh asked, "Has he said anything about Emma?"

Dana wiped her forehead with her arm. "Looky, he doesn't talk to me about his feelin's. Sure, her death has been tough on him, but he's tough. He'll survive."

Mike placed his hand on his hip but waited to speak as the fishermen moved in and grabbed the filled ice chests.

"You know," Mike said, his face taut with frustration, "Jeremy has been named as a person of interest in Emma's murder. The police wish to speak to him, but he has avoided questioning which hasn't made him look good."

Dana placed her hand on her hip, a scowl deepening in the creases of her forehead. "That boy would never."

Raleigh glanced at Mike briefly, a warning in her raised eyebrow. "It's not that we believe Jeremy had anything to do with Emma's death. We just want to talk to him because we think he knows something about what happened, and he may be too scared to tell the truth."

Dana scowled at them. Raleigh could imagine the conflict occurring behind those deep brown eyes. Then the woman sighed. "I don't know anything about Emma's death. I work two jobs now that my husband's gone, so I don't have much time to chase him around." Her lips twisted. "I mean the boy hasn't been home in two nights. Been sleeping at a friend's he says. He's 18, so don't make me out to be the horrible parent here. I do work these two jobs to keep a roof over his head, and he doesn't even appreciate it."

Mike nodded. "Single parenting is difficult. My mom did the best she could, and I'm sure you are as well."

Her frown softened some as she continued to stare at Mike.

Raleigh cleared her throat. "Do you know what friend he has been staying with?" Raleigh could see that Dana was still leery from her furrowed forehead. "We would like to help him, and we can't help him if we can't speak to him."

Dana looked away from them and in the direction of the marina with its line of boats filling the earlier emptier slots. "He's been working for Vinnie Boudreaux for about four months now. Sometimes he just sleeps on the boat."

"Thank you," Mike said. "If Jeremy comes home, please tell him to reach out to us so we can help him."

Dana nodded but turned to help the next customer without a smile.

Raleigh jabbed her head in the direction of the wharf and Mike followed as she walked toward the docks in search of Vinnie's boat.

Mike glanced back at Dana who was looking over a ticket a gentleman in a light blue fishing shirt had handed her. "Do you get the idea that these journalism kids have no one really parenting them?"

Raleigh nodded. "I wouldn't say you can't get into trouble with good parenting though. We managed just fine to get into a mess of trouble."

Mike shrugged, his forehead still crinkled with his deep thoughts. "I guess you're right."

After walking past two neglected boats, they saw an old crewman unloading crates from a fishing boat and stopped to ask if he knew where Vinnie's boat was docked. With his tattered flannel shirt, the old man regarded them suspiciously, but in the end pointed toward a thirty-five-foot shrimp boat about a hundred yards down the dock.

Walking down the wharf, the slips were filled with decaying boats sitting in the smelly lapping fresh water. Several boat decks had men wrapping large rope on the decks and few had men stacking large crates on the dock. Seagulls squawked near the back decks, waiting for the catch to be sorted and their meal to be tossed.

At a shrimp boat trimmed in eggshell blue, a weather-beaten man with flyaway hair in white rubber boots was tossing life vests and netting onto the wharf. He tossed Styrofoam floaters into the pile and then stopped to watch as they approached his keel.

"Vinnie?" Mike questioned, as they sized up the older gentleman. His steel gray hair flapped wildly about in the breeze, and his navy shirt had rips and frays at the edges. He smelled of seaweed, fish, and salt, and Raleigh chose to stand back, hoping to remain upwind.

"Who's askin'?" He grimaced down at the two.

"We're reporters for the Barbeaux Gazette, but we've been volunteering down at the high school, and we were trying to check on Jeremy, a student," Raleigh straightened her shoulders, hoping not to appear intimidated.

Mike glanced her way and then back at Vinnie. "We're real concerned about him, and we were told he's been staying with you."

"That right?" He glared down at them as if they'd catch fire if they were lying.

Raleigh held still without blinking, feeling his suspicions from his overhead position. "His mama told us we might find him here."

Vinnie shook his head, his chin almost touching his chest. "If that woman wouldn't be always making the veiller (vay-yay), she would know where her son was at," he mumbled.

Visiting with all her friends every night. Getting around. That wasn't a French word her Me'Maw or Paw would use very often as they were usually in bed come 7:30.

Mike stepped closer to the keel of the boat, closing in the space. "Actually sir, we are worried that something might happen to him. Two teenagers have turned up dead—two of his friends. We just want to talk to him, make sure he is safe."

Vinnie grunted, turned away from them, and walked down the length of the boat before spryly jumping onto the wharf. She'd pegged him for his sixties, but if she'd been in the ballpark he was in good shape for that age.

"Look, I don't know anything," Vinnie said as he approached, the smell of sweat mixing with fish and seaweed filling the space. "But he has been wound pretty tight lately. I could tell something has been going on. He hasn't been around for two days now, and that's not like him since his mama will be asking for that rent money next week."

Raleigh raised an eyebrow at Mike. He'd been right about the parenting, but it wouldn't help them find Jeremy. He lifted his head in a brief nod but continued looking at Vinnie.

"Did he mention any problems with his girlfriend? Or friends?"

Vinnie hesitated, looking at Mike only. "You know I shouldn't betray his confidences like that. The boy doesn't trust anyone as it is."

Mike shrugged his shoulders. "We just want to help him. We don't have to tell him you told us anything."

Raleigh nodded her agreement.

Vinnie hung his head, and then picked it up and looked into Mike's eyes.

"That week before Emma died, he mentioned at least a hundred times that he thought she was hiding something from him. I said she was cheating, but he said it wasn't like that. He just knew it was something else and the not knowing was driving him crazy. And me having to hear about it."

For a moment, Raleigh thought about all the things a high school girl could hide. Typically, she'd say it revolved around a boy. Jeremy may know something about it that he hadn't told them since he'd kept much from them. "Did he believe she was in danger? Did he mention that at all?"

Vinnie shrugged his muscular shoulders. "He didn't say anything, but he was acting like she could be. You know what I mean? Like he had to be protective of her or something."

Raleigh and Mike exchanged quick glances.

Mike folded his arms across his chest. "Did Jeremy ever mention anyone else? Someone else we could ask about where's he's been?"

Vinnie shook his head, pulling at his tattered shirtsleeve. "The boy's a loner. I gather he never spends much time at school, but I never heard of any friends he'd hang with."

Raleigh handed Vinnie a business card but had to wait for the man's dirty, calloused hand to clasp down on it, as he seemed hesitant. "Please have Jeremy call us if he you see him."

"Or you can call," Mike said.

Vinnie nodded, looking down at the crisp white card in his oil stained hand. "The kid's a good kid. He just hasn't had an easy life. I really hope he isn't in any trouble."

Raleigh smiled. "We hope so, too."

She and Mike turned and walked back down the dock.

"So, something was going on the week before Emma died, and no one seems to be able to tell us exactly what," Mike grumbled so no one could hear.

Raleigh nodded. "I don't believe teenagers keep secrets. I think they just aren't telling us."

"The question is why," Mike said, glancing back at Vinnie who'd walked back around to his boat.

TWENTY-ONE

"I'm just saying," Mike said as he reached for the glass door of Danny's Po-Boys so that Raleigh could enter, "that I wouldn't mind doing a little more cooking if we would stock the house with groceries."

As they walked in, Ms. Dodie Gaspire waved from across the floor, and Raleigh waved back. She hadn't seen the red-haired woman since the last church festival in town, and then the woman had been trying to pawn off these awful looking bits of fudge at a sweet booth.

She focused back on Mike though, not wanting to get distracted into agreeing to anything crazy like cooking every night. "If we don't cook, we don't have dishes. And without a dishwasher, that's a pretty big deal."

He sighed, looking down at her with a classic Mike grin. "That is a fair argument, but this argument isn't done yet."

Raleigh smiled. "That will be pretty hard to beat seeing as neither of us want to wash dishes."

Mike chuckled. "We'll see."

Cindy smiled as they approached the counter. "Well, hello you two. Order will be right up. Take a load off while waiting."

The woman continued on, carrying an overloaded tray of po-boys and fries to a corner booth. The middle age woman had worked at Danny's for as long as Raleigh could remember. As a young girl, on Sunday after church she'd trail behind her Papa to this very same counter where the woman would have their usual order packed and ready to go. Ms. Cindy had been younger then, thinner, and her face firmer. She'd laughed more back then, too.

Mike slid onto a bar stool and took a look around the diner. At 5:30 p.m., only four tables were filled. Usually the senior citizens crowd came in at 4:30 p.m., but the recession had slid into the area years after it had hit everywhere else. Even though the recovery had followed elsewhere, it just didn't seem to be coming here.

"My nephew wants to spend the weekend with me," Mike said, glancing at her as he fiddled with the shiny metal napkin holder. "I told him I'd check with you first."

"Sure," Raleigh said, wondering if this happened often. For her nephew Mason, the newness of sleeping over at Nanan's house had worn off after the first month and then he preferred his Maw's house where his toast bread and coffee milk awaited him on the kitchen counter when he woke up. At Nanan's house it was more of a cereal and milk, pour-your-own-bowl affair.

Still fiddling with the holder, Mike hung his head. "I know this isn't the ideal situation for you. A houseguest, a puppy, and now a kid. Just let me know if it's too much. I can always go and stay with my mom."

Raleigh grinned, "We have shared custody of the canine, so if you leave, custody arrangements will need to be agreed upon."

Mike chuckled.

Raleigh shook her head. "We both know I just take a moment to adjust, especially when kids are involved. This weekend is Me'Maw and Paw's anniversary party. Maybe he'll want to hang with Mason."

"Have you..." Mike trailed off as Lathan Babin walked over to them, a grim look disturbing his boyishly handsome features.

"Sorry to interrupt," he said, reaching out and good-naturedly patting Mike on the back. "It's been a horrendous day with the news about Keith hitting the classroom. The students are devasted as you can imagine. When I saw the two of you, I thought maybe you had something that could begin to make sense of all of this."

Raleigh grimaced. "I don't think anything makes sense when two young people die."

"I know. Such a tragedy." Lathan hung his head. "Are you two investigating the deaths for the paper?"

"As much as we can." Mike shrugged. "When Raleigh finds the bodies, it's a conflict of interest."

Lathan's left eyebrow lifted as he peered at Raleigh with new interest. "How did that happen?" He shook his head. "I mean, we heard Keith was near the boat launch. I didn't take you for the boating type."

Raleigh wasn't sure what he meant by the comment— an insult, a commentary, an observation? She didn't boat though—unless boating turned into a land sport, it wouldn't happen, so she let the remark slide.

"I'm the local Traiteur to the dead," Raleigh said, feeling the heat rise up her throat. Saying it aloud to people made her feel like a freak. It would be easier to announce it to everyone all at once, but then her clientele list might grow to insurmountable proportions.

Again, Lathan's left eyebrow rose. "Sorry, say that again."

To her right, Mike's voice came out gruff, defensive. "The dying seek her out and show her their last moment or their location." He grinned at Raleigh. "She's famous around these parts."

Lathan's forehead furrowed. "I must say as a transplant, I've never heard of such a thing. My instincts are a little skeptical."

Raleigh laughed, and Lathan shifted from one foot to another. "My own instincts fight against the intrusion all the time."

Mike glowered at Lathan. For some reason, Mike felt insulted or infuriated by Lathan's reaction. Raleigh felt it had been better than average.

"Has Jeremy been at school?" Mike asked still glowering but changing the subject.

Lathan shook his head. "Haven't seen him in a week. The students are all talking about it, of course. Theories, rumors, all flying around."

"Such as?" Raleigh asked.

"Oh, just that Keith and Emma may have been intimately involved, and Jeremy took care of both of them. Today I overheard two girls whispering that it was Keith's father. Something about his father caught Emma at the crawfish pond and murdered her, and then Keith threatened to tell on his father, so Leroy killed Keith. There's even a rumor that old Ms. Waters, the history teacher, is killing students who wrote about her for that article on favorite or least favorite teachers. You can imagine where she fell."

Raleigh sighed, gently kicking the bar of the counter with her toes. People loved to be armchair detectives. Rumors very rarely could be substantiated with actual evidence, but some grain of truth usually sparked the tall tale. Finding that grain of sand was what they needed.

Mike tapped on the counter, grimacing at the response. "Anything you think could be true?"

Lathan shrugged. "All I know about my students outside of school is what they share with me. Emma never spoke about any troubles, and Keith, well, he worried about his dad a bit, but I don't know if I would say it was to the extreme of murder."

Raleigh and Mike had spent only a few weeks in the class getting their program started, so they knew the teenagers spoke about their lives, but sometimes you had to prod if you wanted them to really talk about anything that truly mattered. Class time wasn't conducive for this, so Lathan probably hadn't heard much.

Cindy placed a white to-go bag in front of Raleigh. "Here y'all go. Sorry 'bout the wait, but we're down a kitchen staff worker. If you know anyone who's looking for a job, send them our way."

They thanked her, and Raleigh slid off the barstool causing Lathan to take a step back.

"Well, thanks for the news," Lathan said. "Even if it is grim, it makes facing these kids tomorrow a little easier."

Mike shook his extended hand and remained quiet. Raleigh knew something was going on behind those green eyes.

Lathan's eyes slid over her again as they said good-bye. Raleigh had surmised from his lack of attention at Madison's mixer that she wasn't his type. This did not bother her in the least, but she'd over-heard the students in class talking about how Mr. Babin needed a relationship, and she wondered if women really were his type since he never seemed to date—at least according to school gossip (but they all knew how accurate that was). She'd watched him speaking to the women at the party, but Madison had reported no matches for him at the end of the night.

Back in the Jeep, Raleigh placed the warm bag of food on her lap and thought about all the gossip they'd heard along the way. So far it had all been a dead end.

Or had it?

It was difficult to substantiate gossip when forced to verify it from people who gossiped.

"Do you think that Lathan doesn't find me attractive because he's a closet gay man or I'm not his type?" Raleigh said, thinking about all the gossip surrounding the teachers.

"What?" Mike asked alarmed. "Where does that come from?"

Raleigh shrugged. "Just considering all the gossip. I mean, how do you really verify truth in gossip?"

Mike settled back into his seat and grew pensive. "Well, what makes you think he's not attracted to you?"

Raleigh waved her hand to dismiss the idea. "He barely notices me. Single people our age in Barbeaux Bayou who aren't on drugs, divorced, or looking twenty years older are a very small pool at this point. Usually most men show at least some interest just because the pickings are from a shallow pond. It's the same for women. We have to eliminate so many that the prospects all get at least a second look."

Mike chuckled, a hearty sound. "Don't forget to eliminate the crazy. I have found that this makes the pool almost nonexistent. I'm with you though. Maybe he does have a different sexual preference and doesn't want his students to know."

That could be one reason, among so many others.

"If a teacher is having an affair with a student, what teacher would you suspect?"

Mike raised an eyebrow with a smirk. "Mrs. Waters?"

Raleigh laughed, but then shuddered. "Uh, no. Mrs. Waters is probably older than my father. She's been teaching 42 years at this point. Who teaches that long anymore?"

Mike shook his head, his eyes wide in disbelief. "I don't know anyone who could handle teenagers that long. After only a few weeks of attitudes, I'm ready to go back to our newsroom full-time."

Raleigh chuckled, agreeing silently. Madison offered more than her fair share of attitude; Raleigh didn't need more. Mike pulled the Jeep into the shell driveway behind her silver coupe that she rarely seemed to use these days. The two had slid into old habits from high school, with Mike chauffeuring her around town in the Jeep, but the vehicle was now twenty years old. Mike had to perform regular maintenance, but the reality was that if they continued to use it every day, they'd eventually put an end to this high school relic.

Mike shut the engine and furrowed his eyebrows. "I hear something."

With her fingers on the handle, Raleigh paused to listen to the churning motor sound coming from behind the house for the second time this week. Except this sounded more like farm equipment, a sound from her childhood.

Raleigh lurched out of the vehicle. "What the hell?"

Fumbling with the latch of the metal gate of her fence, Raleigh stumbled through the yard, noticing her newly cut grass along the way.

Around back, Paw pushed a yellow tiller through a newly plowed section in the far-right quadrant, his stooped form pushing forward as the metal blades left behind fine granules of grey dirt.

Stopping short, she stared at the patch of dirt as the puppy tripped over its feet in its bounce toward the two of them. Mike swept her up as she looped around his legs.

Paw glanced off in their direction and shut the tiller off. The air echoed with the silence, and Raleigh's ears struggled to adapt.

"Hey girl," he said, wiping his hands along his blue Dickie pants. "I thought you might like a little garden of your own."

Raleigh smiled, feeling it rise up through her entire face. She finished the walk and stood at the edge of the five neat rows. This would be hers—just like the ones she'd spent her childhood running through. She wouldn't even think about all the houseplants she'd killed over the years. She could learn anything. Like Sue Ann had said: Cheramie women could do anything. Okay, she was paraphrasing. Sue Ann had probably meant that Cheramie women were crazy.

Leaning over, Raleigh unzipped her boots. As she pulled them off, Paw chuckled.

"Never understood why you had to feel the dirt with your toes."

Stepping into the dirt with her bare feet, the coolness seeped in and the coarseness imprinted under her smooth instep.

With that first step, she was six years old, running through Paw's garden with her pockets full of seeds that he'd told her to carry for him. Seeds that meant life—not the death she was used to these days. Maybe it was possible to have both—life and death—if she balanced carefully.

Glancing back at Mike, she watched him hand Paw a beer can. It must be from Mike's stash. In her complete enthrallment, she'd missed Mike opening the back door and bringing out Me'Maw's forbidden vice.

She stepped even further into the dirt and decided she could let this one go. Mike and Paw could have their beer, and Me'Maw would forgive them all one more time. She didn't want to ruin the moment.

TWENTY-TWO

Funeral appearances were like calling a seance in the middle of a cemetery and having all the spirits fight to come through. Raleigh avoided cemeteries and funerals like people avoided lines at the bar restrooms—she only went when absolutely required, under dire distress.

A teenager's funeral certainly equaled distress.

Emma's casket had been closed, but Raleigh could feel a disturbance from the nether regions of the church. Every muscle in her body tensed against the intrusion.

"I don't think Jeremy's coming," Mike whispered. The two had sat next to each other through the mass and now stood back as the last rites were bestowed.

Raleigh shook her head. "Half the high school is here today, but no sign of the boyfriend—strange."

A balding man with a reddish-brown mustache in a ratty black t-shirt turned slightly, glancing at them.

"Maybe we just missed him somewhere," Mike leaned down again and whispered.

"Nah, dude," the stranger stepped back and whispered. "My

sister has people to keep him away. A couple of people weren't invited." He chuckled. "My sister is ruthless."

Mike and Raleigh exchanged glances. Mike leaned forward as they received dirty looks from a neighboring couple. "Who else couldn't attend?"

"Uncle Agnus for sure." The stranger grinned. "The crazy loon always was inappropriate with the ladies of the family. Also, some of her friends were told not to attend because a detective told my sister that they weren't helping the police with the investigation."

Raleigh scanned the faces of the high school group gathered again. Olivia's red hair did not appear among the group. Had Emma's mother judged Olivia as inappropriate to attend her best friend's funeral?

From her lack of appearance, it would seem so.

Mike squeezed her hand. Their signal for a hasty escape as he knew how these things made her feel. They took a few steps to the side and disappeared behind a neighboring mausoleum structure.

As they did so, she spotted a familiar spatter of brown hair and skinny arms around the corner.

"Jeremy," she hissed.

Mike stepped forward. "Jeremy, we just want to talk to you."

"Nah," Jeremy said, swiping at tears trailing down his cheek, a look of surprise etched in his eyes. "I heard about this talk. Y'all need to leave my people alone."

Raleigh stepped closer as he looked braced to run. "We need to hear your side so we can help you."

"Help put me in jail?" Jeremy said. "Well, I didn't do anything. I should have. I should have stopped her from going off alone that night."

"To who?" Raleigh asked. "Who was Emma going meet?"

Jeremy took a step back. "Ask Olivia. Emma kept going on about how she needed to help her, save her."

"What do you know about it?" Mike said, gesturing his hand in a downward motion meant to calm.

Jeremy shrugged. "You two are so smart, why do you need me?"

Raleigh said, "Don't you want to help us find out the truth? If you aren't in the wrong that is?"

"Everyone's guilty of something," Jeremy said, squeezing his fists. "I got angry and did something bad." Another tear rolled down his cheek as his lip curled up. "But I would never hurt Emma."

Jeremy turned to leave.

"Are you sure it's Olivia?" Raleigh called after him. "How do you know?"

Jeremy paused in his brisk walk. "Emma texted Olivia to meet her that night right after we left."

Mike and Raleigh let him go as he hurried away.

"So, we move back to Olivia," Raleigh said.

Mike frowned. "I feel like we need to get all these kids in a room and interrogate them."

Raleigh smirked. "Like herding cats."

Mike nodded.

Later that night, Raleigh tossed the comforter off and blew her hair from her face in frustration. She couldn't sleep and she felt minutes ticking by that would leave her with raccoon eyes and terse feelings in the morning. Funerals left her restless, and her brain would not stop running over Mike's house fire and Emma's and Keith's deaths. She couldn't help but feel as though she had all the pieces to put the puzzle together, but she couldn't see the emerging pattern. Frustration and guilt gnawed at her and made sleep elusive.

Then there was Mike. She felt a decisive conclusion needed to be drawn about this whole friendship-romance. She couldn't handle this turmoil any longer.

As long as all of these thoughts were ping-ponging around in her brain, sleep would not come.

A throaty attempt at a whisper came from the foot of the stairs. "Raleigh Lynn."

The tone and failure at a low volume told her that Aunt Clarice had come for a visit in the middle of the night—her first since Mike had taken up residence downstairs ten feet from the bottom of those stairs.

Sprinting from the bed, Raleigh snatched her robe from the floor and hurried downstairs. Thankfully, Aunt Clarice had stayed away since Mike had moved in deviating from her regular visiting schedule. Raleigh had been appreciative, thinking that a ghost appearing in the living room might be too much for even an understanding guy like Mike. People had limits to what they could live with, especially while they slept vulnerable in bed at night.

Appearing in her young thirty something form in a gray, wool pencil skirt and frilly pink blouse, Aunt Clarice braced herself against the archway of the living room with a hip jutting out just enough to hint at the sexiness she'd been in her life. Her pin up curls and red lipstick perfectly in place as they had been in real life up until the last two weeks of her illness when the effort had been too much.

In greeting, Aunt Clarice waved a cigarette hand in the air, and Raleigh couldn't help but roll her eyes. The woman was incorrigible.

A faint shimmer next to Aunt Clarice's smirking form caught Raleigh's eye and slowly a new shadowy figure began to emerge. An older lady, hunched over with graying hair pulled back tightly in a bun at the base of her neck, peered shyly at her from under long black eyelashes and a makeup free face. The older woman continued wringing her hands against a white apron covering a black gingham dress.

Her form wasn't as solid as Aunt Clarice's, and as the older woman glanced nervously between Raleigh and Aunt Clarice, her form flickered as if a light bulb was on the blink.

"What is going on?" Raleigh hissed, glancing behind her at Mike's closed bedroom door.

"Dear," Aunt Clarice said, tilting her head, "I mentioned that Dora needed your help."

Raleigh tried to remember if that was true or one of Aunt Clarice's stretches of the truth, but she had so much on her mind she

couldn't recollect at this late hour with no sleep and full on panic that
Mike would walk into this mess.

Raleigh waved her hand in the direction of Mike's room. "It's a
really bad time."

Aunt Clarice pouted her lips. "Well, dear, I live here, too. Afterall, it's my house, and I've tried to be respectful for a time. But I think
it is time you just introduce us and be done with it."

Raleigh glared at her. "That might be easier if you hadn't brought
a houseguest."

Aunt Clarice chuckled, her rich, throaty laugh that always
sounded like dark chocolate candy indulgence. "This will be quick.
She has a message for her granddaughter."

The older woman, Dora, perked up, her form becoming more
solid. "You know my granddaughter Evie?"

Raleigh shrugged, feeling the moments tick by where Mike could
walk in and have both of their hearts lurching into their throats.
"What is Evie's last name?"

The old woman looked hopeful. "Evie Cantrell. Do you know
her?"

"I will find her," Raleigh said. "What is your message?"

Dora looked to Aunt Clarice; her eyes filled with doubt a she
wrung the apron harder between her fingers.

Aunt Clarice jabbed her chin up. "Like I told you Dora, you can
trust my niece. She does this for a living." At this, Aunt Clarice
winked a heavily mascaraed eye at Raleigh. What Raleigh did for a
living was write for the Barbeaux Gazette; what she did because of a
pestering family inheritance was take down messages from ghosts in
the middle of the night. There was a distinct difference.

Dora's head bobbed up and down. "I need you to tell my granddaughter that she was adopted. Her dad is not her dad, so it's okay
that she feels the way she does about him. I need you to make my
daughter tell Evie the truth so that she can meet her real dad before it
is too late. He's sick."

Raleigh raised an eyebrow at Aunt Clarice. This did not sound like drama she wanted to dip herself into as she actively tried to avoid interfering and getting involved with the living.

Aunt Clarice raised a penciled-in eyebrow and seemed to dare Raleigh to object. The woman would probably have a noisy party every night for a week in retaliation.

"Does your daughter know Evie's real dad?" Raleigh asked, sighing as she thought about all the ways this could go wrong. "Will she want Evie to know the truth?"

Dora bunched her apron tighter. "She's just scared, but Evie is in trouble. My girl needs the truth before she does something destructive."

Aunt Clarice flipped her hand back and looked at the older woman with disapproval. "Dora haunts her family. She can't bear to leave them, but of course they can't hear her."

"What the hell?" Mike said.

Raleigh jumped, startled. As she turned to see his bare chest standing in the doorway, she realized she'd stopped looking for him briefly. He gawked at the two corporeal figures standing in the archway, his eyes large circles.

Dora whimpered and then faded away.

"Well, hello, hun," Aunt Clarice said, smiling. "I have to say, I didn't think you were going to grow into such a strapping young man when you were running into my house trying to get Raleigh to go fulfill whatever harebrained plan the two of you had dreamed up."

Mike's forehead crinkled as he puzzled over the thirty-year-old form of Raleigh's aunt. "Aunt Clarice?"

Aunt Clarice curtsied. "In the flesh, so to speak, as they say."

Mike gawked and his sun-kissed flesh paled several shades as he swallowed against what Raleigh could only infer was panic.

"Tell Dora I will speak to her granddaughter." Raleigh rushed out, feeling she needed to move this along before Mike's reaction worsened as the reality of the situation registered. "I don't know what the situation is with the family, but I will give it a try."

Aunt Clarice nodded, her smirk telling Raleigh she knew that

Mike was bothered. "The woman needs to let go, but she's afraid Evie will hurt herself. Do what you can, doll."

She blew air kisses before fading away.

Mike leaned against his bedroom doorframe. "That's not normal."

Raleigh grimaced. "I know. She and I have an agreement. She doesn't intrude on my space."

Mike pointed to the spot where Aunt Clarice had just shimmered out. "But she was standing right there. And I saw her." He squinted at Raleigh. "How did I see her?"

Raleigh shrugged. She hadn't thought about him not being able to see her. Maybe that should have been her first thought since not everyone connected to the dying or saw ghosts. "Usually Aunt Clarice's nights are Sundays, but she's stayed away out of respect for you, but I guess anyone can see a ghost if they are open to it."

As she said it though, she thought about how Amber had been unable to see Aunt Clarice. Had that been her devilish Aunt's choice?

Mike shuddered. "I don't know if I want to."

Raleigh grimaced. "I know. I just keep waiting for you to decide it's too much. I mean, I can't get away from the freakiness of my life, but you... you can walk away whenever it's too much. And who could blame you? I mean, none of this is normal."

Raleigh's pitch rose an octave, her face burned, and she realized she was rambling and delirious. It was past midnight, she hadn't fallen asleep, and her brain was exhausted from trying to string the answers together from the sparse bits and pieces they'd managed.

Mike stepped forward, his coloring slowly returning. "You're waiting for me to walk away?"

Waving her hands in the air, Raleigh squealed in frustration. "Who wouldn't? I mean, this is all a mess. You just walked in on an SOS call from a ghost. Who wants to deal with that in a relationship or friendship or I don't even know anymore what we have? It's just one more weird thing in my life that I can't ask anyone else to carry."

Mike frowned. "Is that why you haven't been ready to date? Do you think I'm going to just walk away from you?"

From his softened eyes and drawn mouth, she knew she'd offended him or hurt his feelings or both. She hadn't intended to, but she could feel all the frustration swelling inside of her.

Raleigh gripped the post of the staircase with enough strength to hold herself up. "What if it doesn't work out? What happens if we don't have any chemistry and it's awkward? What happens if we screw it up? I can't imagine not having you in my life and failed relationships don't typically end in friendship. I should know. I have a few to give as examples."

Closing up the space between them, Mike lifted her off the top step of the staircase and pulled her into him. He covered her lips with his, and she felt the soft press of his lips and the searing heat build between them as she felt the nearness of his body pressed against hers and his arms squeezing her. Her resistance melted and she leaned into him. A feeling of comfort flowed through her, but also the kindling of a fire that matched the security.

Pulling away, his eyes stared into hers, searching for a response.

He grinned. "I don't think chemistry will be a problem."

With cheeks burning, Raleigh laughed. "But it's such a risk..."

Mike pulled her back in, quieting her with another deep, longing kiss, more insistent than the last.

When he pulled away, she couldn't catch her breath.

Mike stared into her eyes. "Everything is a risk, Ree, but think about the reward."

Raleigh felt a small tug of resistance, a fear that she'd lose him forever if she couldn't get this right. She didn't have the best track record, and she already had one failed engagement to her name. "Are you sure?"

He touched his forehead to hers. "It's time for us."

TWENTY-THREE

Raleigh lifted the heavy Magnalite pot over her head and slid it back into its place in the top cabinet. Me'Maw's cabinets had been lovingly built, if not masterly crafted. Her grandparents had built this house with cash as they'd socked money away for years while they lived in a three-room house. They'd had their eldest son Davey in that old shack, but by the time Uncle Jude had come along, Paw had completed the framing of the outside and they'd moved in, living in it as they'd put in floors and cabinets little by little as the mechanic work and garden had brought in income. The house had history, and even the wood from the three-room shack had been utilized in the construction of this home.

Me'Maw paused in her stirring. "Thanks for helping me. When Ms. Louise got sick, I didn't know how I'd get all of this cooking done for the church family dinner tonight."

Raleigh swept over the room, looking for more dirty dishes, and surmised that she'd cleaned and put away everything so far, some of the pots twice. "No problem, Me'Maw. I needed a bit of a distraction this afternoon anyway."

"Oh?" Me'Maw fixed her eyes on Raleigh sideways from the large pot of white beans.

Raleigh leaned against the fork drawer, her feet aching from the standing. "Teenagers dying and Mike's house fire has my brain spinning. I'm trying to put it all together."

Me'Maw placed the spoon in the wooden spoon rest next to the stove. "Are you and Mike having trouble?"

Raleigh twiddled with the old milk jar of peanuts Paw kept on the counter. "Not trouble exactly. Just uncertainties. Aunt Clarice didn't help by showing up with another ghost last night."

Me'Maw shook her head as her feet shuffled in her slippers toward her old wood rocking chair. "Now that's a woman who enjoyed causing trouble, but I'm sure Mike will be okay with all of it. He's a good soul."

Raleigh stared down at the worn linoleum tile. "I just can't help but feel that he will grow tired of all this."

On the table, Me'Maw's fingers caressed her deck of cards. "Not everyone does, Raleigh Lynn. Good men accept all that you have to offer, even the things that aren't so pretty all the time."

Me'Maw had never really steered her wrong in life but getting dating advice from someone in her 80s who'd met her husband at seventeen didn't feel like the wisest decision. Mike was good stock as Paw would say though, and he did seem to be all in. Her cautious nature had led her to insist they take it slow—try a date first. Mike had laughed, but he'd said he could make that happen. He hadn't said when though, and today they'd gone to work and been completely normal. Raleigh didn't know what to do with that.

The screen door slapped, and tiny nails tapped against the floor as Luna bounded in leaps ahead of Paw. She rushed over to Raleigh's legs and sniffed around her feet.

Paw rubbed his hands on a towel. "I thought I'd wear her out in the garden, but I think it was the other way around. I forgot how much energy a puppy has."

Raleigh laughed as the puppy stretched her paws out against her legs, a sign that she wanted to be picked up. Now that she'd settled in and didn't spend the entire night whining, Raleigh felt more generous towards her.

Besides, the puppy was lonesome without Mike, her afternoon companion, as he'd gone help Nick out on a new home construction site.

Raleigh swooped her up and Luna burrowed into her chest. She smelled like puppy and dirt. Probably the same smell Raleigh had emitted when she was younger coming in from Paw's garden.

The door swung open again, and Joey stomped his boots on Me'Maw's rug. "It sure is smelling good in here, Me'Maw."

Me'Maw beamed. "Well, hello Joey. Did you eat? Are you on a break at work?"

Joey removed his cap and placed it on the counter as he continued into the kitchen. "No, I was helping daddy with that old tractor again, but I came looking for Raleigh."

"Oh, yeah?" Paw said, turning from the sink. "I hope for friendly reasons."

Joey nodded. "Yes, sir. I want to talk this case over with her. I thought maybe talking it out loud might make things settle for me. 'Cause to tell you the truth, I'm having trouble getting the pieces to fall into place in any way that makes sense."

Paw lumbered toward his chair, his limp more pronounced today. "Well, have a seat. Always better to have more brains working on it."

Raleigh could tell that Paw couldn't wait to hear about the case. He loved discussing the news and was up to speed with everything going on in town as many of his old friends had breakfast at least three times a week to discuss the town, although it was their sons and grandson's that ran it now. The high school might be a stretch, but if you wanted to know about the town council or the people in town, Paw had the word.

Joey claimed a spot, leaning against the sink, where he crossed his leg over and leaned his elbow on the counter. "Sheriff has decided that Jeremy Garcia is the top suspect in both murders, and he wants me to bring him in."

Raleigh sank into one of the chairs. "The evidence is nothing more than circumstantial against him. How will the sheriff charge him?"

Joey shrugged. "I don't think he really cares. He feels the pressure to close the case with two dead kids and he's grasping for it not to be a PR nightmare."

Paw rapped his knuckles on the table. "Dead kids don't look good, especially without a suspect, and his reelection campaign is gearing up. Not usually the best time for good, honest police work."

Joey's head bobbed up and down. "I don't have another suspect though. I keep going over the details, and no one stands out."

Me'Maw's rocker creaked as she rocked back and forth, but she remained quiet.

Raleigh leaned forward, bracing her elbows on her knees. "Let's run it through. Emma's body was dumped at Leroy's crawfish pond, which happens to be Keith's father, who later turns up dead at the canal boat launch."

Joey shifted his position. "Both suffered trauma to their heads, but ultimately the cause of death was drowning. The weapon was undetermined but created enough force to pierce the skin and leave a head wound. It's likely they were knocked out and then drowned without gaining consciousness."

Paw grunted. "Lucky for them."

"The canal has easy access," Raleigh said, chewing on her bottom lip as her thoughts worked themselves out in her head. "But Leroy's crawfish ponds are out of the way and typically locked."

Joey nodded. "Keith forgot to lock up the night Emma was dumped—or did he? He could have been a part of whatever this is and then he was killed later when he threatened to give it all up?"

Leaning back, Raleigh thought about how the pieces would lie if that were the case. "If we are talking kids, that doesn't clear Jeremy.

That bracelet belonged to his cousin and it was found on Emma's body."

"And the bracelet has been a dead end so far. There was never a suspect in the cousin's death, but she was also close to Jeremy. I have a picture of the bracelet for you today. The reigns on evidence have grown tighter these days."

Raleigh let the comment slide in front of her grandparents, knowing that he must have had some trouble over bringing her the bracelet. And the only way that anyone would know this would be Max. "As a suspect, Jeremy is questionable because he's acting like a person determined to find a killer on his own. He told Mike and I yesterday that Emma was going to meet Olivia right before she was murdered."

Joey roused his head. "Well that would add her as a person of interest, especially since she hasn't been forthcoming herself."

Paw rapped his knuckles on the table again. "Everything might point to Jeremy, but teenagers aren't this good at keeping secrets. Maybe from their parents for a while, but not everyone they know. They jabber on and on to puff themselves up."

Raleigh chewed on her inner lip. Paw was right. They had to have shared what was going on with someone.

"You know," Raleigh said, "they have been saying that Emma was acting strange before she died, trying to control everyone. Jeremy told Vinnie that Emma was scared. Keith got into a fight with Jeremy. That wasn't typical of Keith."

Joey nodded slowly. "So, Keith may have known something that Jeremy wanted to know."

Raleigh said, "So, what we really need to know is who would they talk to?"

Paw leaned forward. "We could drop in on Ol' Leroy and ask. I've been meaning to stop by with my condolences."

Raleigh nodded. "I've been wanting to talk with him again. I think we need to know who Keith has taken to the crawfish ponds previously."

Joey nodded slowly, his eyes narrowing. "That would narrow our suspect list."

Paw rose. "Let's go then. It'll be just one family stopping to check in on another."

Raleigh hid her grin as she followed Paw out the door. Joey grabbed his cap, looking worried. One family checking on another wasn't simple under Sheriff Breaux's command, she supposed.

Fifteen minutes later, Joey had pulled his old truck up under a tree next to a grungy white cottage set back among trees and palm bushes. A rusted, green metal glider rocker sat on the porch with a pristine welcome rug, but patches of grass had given way to dirt spots around the yard, giving off the illusion that they'd stepped back into the times of plow farming and horseback arrivals.

Ol' Leroy sat on the front stoop, polishing a pair of shoes and peering at them as they approached. From the bristly facial hair and stringy hair on his head as well as the shallow pallor of his skin, Raleigh did not need to ask how he was dealing with the death of his only child.

"Leroy," Paw said, coming to a stop before the man. "We've come to pay our respects to your family. To express our sympathies."

Leroy nodded, continuing with the rubbing of the shoe. "Darlene says I need to have shiny shoes for the funeral. I don't know why. My boy never saw me in shiny shoes before." His voice cracked and he lowered his head.

Paw sank down next to him on the stoop. "It's putting our best self forward for the person that we love, showing them the pride we have that the Lord allowed them in our lives for even a small amount of time."

Leroy nodded; his shoulders hunched. "I don't know what I'm going to do without him."

Paw squeezed the younger man's shoulder. "You have a wife and a farm to run. We get up every day and put one foot forward, trusting that we will find our way."

Leroy grunted. "The ponds are in trouble now. I had a contract with the seafood shed, but they don't want my crawfish right now on account of the dead girl. They say people will object to eating my crawfish. You tell me, how would they even know?"

Raleigh swallowed. Poor Leroy's life was not going well right now. It really put issues in perspective.

Joey shook his head. "Then advertise. It's peak season, and everyone always wants crawfish. Sell it yourself."

Leroy shrugged. "I have 400 acres. I know that sounds like a lot, but the big to-dos have 4,000 acres. I don't keep up with them, but I've been able to get by. My granddaddy planted these fields and so did my daddy. I turned them into crawfish ponds, of course. That's where the money was, but who will I pass it onto now?"

"Did Keith want to be a crawfish farmer?" Raleigh asked, trying to picture the quiet kid with headphones always in his ears doing the backbreaking work of lugging 40-pound crawfish sacks from the pond every day.

"Of course not," Leroy said, shaking his head. "He wanted to be some kind of artist. I didn't want to be a farmer when I was his age either, but then I grew up. He would have done ran this place."

Raleigh frowned. Keith had drawn a comic for the last two news-papers, and he'd been really good.

Joey cleared his throat. "Did you know Keith's friends? Possibly any of them that would have hung out here?"

Leroy shook his head. "No one came here because it meant they had to work. Well the Garcia boy didn't mind the work if I gave him a few dollars. Keith's girlfriend came to the place all the time. Darlene didn't like the girl none, says she wasn't good enough for our boy."

"Oh yeah?" Raleigh asked, thinking about mother's intuition of teenagers.

Leroy shrugged. "We still haven't heard from her. My wife is a good judge of character."

Raleigh nodded. Olivia had avoided Keith's parents, but for what reason. Possibly a guilty conscience or fear that someone was killing her friends and she could be next. At this point, Raleigh couldn't form an assumption.

Paw patted Leroy's knee. "If you need anything, give me or Alcee a call. Your daddy helped me through my son's funeral, so I can do the same."

Leroy nodded and Paw struggled to his feet.

Leroy continued polishing the already shiny black shoe as they returned to the old truck. Raleigh wished she had something to tell him that would make him feel better, but Keith's last thoughts had been that Olivia had betrayed him. Jeremy said that Olivia had spoken to Emma last. Had his son been killed by his girlfriend? Raleigh had lived through this in high school when Katherine, her best friend, had been killed by her boyfriend, so she couldn't say that it was impossible.

Back in the truck, Joey said, "Olivia, the girlfriend, has not been willing to say much of anything to us. She's been evasive."

Raleigh nodded. "Maybe I can get her to talk."

"You think?" Joey asked, glancing at her in the middle. Paw sat against the door, looking out the window as the trees and blue sky passed by.

"I'm going to use what we know." Raleigh shrugged. "Besides, I want to show the picture of that bracelet to a few teachers at school. Courtney's sister said she never went anywhere. She may have received it or stolen it from someone at school."

Joey looked at the road ahead. "Let me know if someone seems suspicious with their answers. I can look into it."

Paw glanced toward them. "Glad to hear the Cheramies working on the right side of the law. It's too bad we have the wrong sheriff in office, running unopposed at that."

Raleigh forced her lips down from a smile. Someone must have mentioned to him that Joey was considering running for sheriff.

"Yes, sir," Raleigh said. "Such a shame we don't have a good person running for office."

TWENTY-FOUR

In the B hall of the school, Raleigh paused by the mural of the school mascot bursting from the fifty-yard line of the Barbeaux High football field. When Raleigh had attended over ten years ago, these walls had been plain white bricks. Of course, that was back when she and Mike had been students trolling around with heavy backpacks and even bigger attitudes. The hairstyles and slang had changed, but the attitude size had remained the same.

Raleigh watched the faux wood door for movement. "So, what's the plan?"

Mike swung his hair out of his face. "You talk to Olivia, and I'll speak to Lathan. Maybe the students have told him something useful. He may recognize the bracelet in the picture and give us another lead."

Raleigh nodded, her mind running over ways to get a teenage girl to tell the truth. She had nothing. "Got it."

After knocking on the door, they waited for someone to open it from the inside. All of the classrooms in the school were equipped with self-locking doors as a safety precaution. It made it difficult to slip inside without causing a disturbance, but in today's world, everyone saw it as a necessary inconvenience.

Dex opened the door, gave a curt half-smile, and then pushed his chair back toward a table, all without standing up. Multi-talented, that one.

Leaning over a student, Lathan pointed out something on a computer screen. As they walked in, he looked up. "Ah, the professionals have arrived, people. These students are experiencing the crunch of a deadline right now and could use some assistance. If you'd get Megan over there to show you the layout so far, that would be fantastic."

From a computer screen in the back corner of the classroom, a frenzied Megan looked up with anxiety circles across her forehead. Raleigh recognized the look as the one they wore on their own weekly deadline.

Mike looked at her and grinned. "I got Megan." He nodded his head in the direction of Olivia as he raised an eyebrow. "She looks like she needs you."

Looking toward Olivia, Raleigh noticed half a dozen balled up papers on the girl's table area and a pencil tapping to match her furrowed eyebrows.

As she approached, Raleigh glanced down at the two sentences Olivia had written about the spring pirogue charity event and sighed. No matter where she went, she couldn't avoid community involvement stories.

Olivia huffed, her green eyes flashing. "I hate this story."

Raleigh eased down into the blue metal chair next to her. "I can't say I enjoy writing about these things either."

"Ugh!" she mumbled. "Why do we cover these silly stories?"

Raleigh shrugged. "Because high schools don't want to get sued for stories about what's really in the lunch special or who got caught smoking a Juul in the bathroom this month."

She laughed. The pencil stopped thumping, and she leaned back in her chair. "I can see the vein in Mr. Babin's temple throbbing from even the mere suggestion of a story about the latest sexual statistics among freshmen and why our school pregnancy rates are so high."

"A girl after my own heart." Raleigh grinned. "On some level, Mike and I are partly responsible for some of those restrictions."

Olivia's eyes widened. "So all those stories my mama told me were true?"

Raleigh laughed, wondering who her mama was and if she should be mortified or offended. "I guess that depends on what version she told you. There were plenty stories going around after a story almost got us killed. Correction, one of my best friends did die."

"That sounds cool." Olivia's eyes grew even larger and her mouth opened a bit. "Writing about this is so lame though."

Raleigh shrugged. "What would happen though if you wrote about Emma and Keith? Not as a memorial, but about what happened to them? What will that do to the school? To their friends?"

Olivia's eyebrows furrowed together. "But shouldn't we be allowed to write it since it matters? It's news."

Raleigh tilted her head. "What would this story say that would help your fellow students?"

"Maybe that people don't know what really happened to them," Olivia said. "Maybe that people should stop pretending that they know the truth and that Emma and Keith spilled all their secrets to them."

"Secrets?" Raleigh asked, nonchalantly, seeing her way into this conversation.

"Yes," a voice behind them said. "There are plenty secrets around this school."

Turning in the chair, Raleigh faced Jeremy who fidgeted with his hands in the front pocket of a hoodie. With greasy hair, dirt stained jeans, and eyes darting around the room, he appeared bedraggled and anxious. Once a well-groomed young man, the murders had taken a toll on him internally and externally.

"Jeremy," Raleigh said loudly over the din of voices around them.

"Would you like to join our conversation? We've been wanting to talk to you."

"Oh, yeah?" Jeremy spit out. "Why? So, you can pin it all on me and wrap it all up pretty?"

Pushing the chair back, Raleigh stood, keeping him in her sight the entire movement. "Jeremy, all we want is to talk to you. We didn't say you had anything to do with your friends dying."

Jeremy pushed out a forced laugh. "They didn't just die, right, Olivia?"

"What?" Olivia asked as if she'd been prodded with an electric pulse.

Mr. Babin turned, his eyes flickering a moment of recognition before he stepped toward them. "How did you get in here?" He glanced toward the door, and everyone's eyes snapped to the open door.

"Sorry, Mr. Babin," Dex said. He leaned over from his chair by the door and pushed the door closed. Locks meant nothing if someone opened the door every knock.

Lathan cleared his throat. "Jeremy, you can't be in this class. What class do you have this period?"

Jeremy bucked up. "Trying to get rid of me, Mr. Babin? I bet you would want that."

Lathan began to color in the face. "Do I need to get an administrator in here to talk to you?"

Jeremy reached into his hoodie pocket and returned with a small black handgun.

A sharp, collective gasp went up amongst the eleven students and then silence fell as all eyes watched him.

With a quick, darting glance, Raleigh got her bearings of the room. Mike stood five feet behind her with two students hiding behind him. Other students sat mounted in their seats unable to move. Standing in front of Olivia's table, she could hear Jeremy's breath in his chest they were so close. She could not move without drawing attention to the move itself.

Jeremy waved the black Beretta wildly in the air, his eyes as cold as the metal. "Why don't we get a few things straight before you call administration. I want them to have the whole picture when they get here."

Mr. Babin raised his hands. "Now, listen. I'm sure you don't want to do this. Situations like these don't end well, and you should want so much more than this for yourself."

"Olivia tell us about that night," Jeremy said, ignoring the teacher. "Emma texted you. I know she did. I saw the message."

Olivia whimpered. "No, she didn't."

Jeremy jabbed the gun in her direction. "Don't lie to me." Olivia's shoulders jumped and tensed up. Her chin trembled. "Emma wanted you to meet her. She wanted to talk to you."

Olivia's eyes darted to Raleigh, and Raleigh saw the fear clouding her hazel eyes.

She pleaded. "I swear I didn't see her that night."

Jeremy raised the gun in the air and gripped his head with his palms. "Stop lying to me. You are nothing but a liar, and Keith paid for your lies. Don't you think you owe him the truth; Emma the truth?"

Tears sprang to Olivia's eyes. She seemed to shrink into the chair. "Keith was not my fault."

Raleigh raised her hand to try and calm the situation. "Jeremy, why don't you tell us what you are thinking so we can get this all sorted out. We all want to know the truth."

Jeremy jabbed the gun toward Olivia. "Emma met her that night because Emma was worried about her stupid decisions. Emma wouldn't tell me what she meant by stupid decisions, but it is amazing what you can find out by disappearing."

He glared at Olivia, and Raleigh shifted from her left to her right foot to draw his attention away from the girl. "What did you find out?"

"Keith told me about his own suspicions, you know?" Jeremy smirked, his movements jerky as he shifted around in front of them.

"You weren't as clever as you thought you were. If you wanted to keep things secret, you should have kept your normal routine up. If you cancel date after date with the guy that is your boyfriend and then skip out on your friends, people start to look closer at what you are doing and who you are doing it with."

At this, he glanced at Lathan Babin who hadn't moved. His pained expression revealed his dilemma over what he should do. Raleigh supposed teacher training didn't include hostage negotiation.

Olivia began to tremble next to Raleigh. "You are embarrassing yourself, Jeremy. You need to stop this."

Anger darkened his face and he stepped up until he was touching the table. Raleigh held her breath. "Do you even know how to tell the truth?" He jabbed the gun in her face, three inches from her nose. "Your friends are dead, and you are worried about embarrassment?"

"Just tell him," a hysterical voice called from the back corner of the room. "We have all been talking about it."

Lathan stepped forward. "I don't think we need to be airing Olivia's business out in front of everyone. Why don't we let everyone leave, Jeremy, and you and I talk about it?"

Jeremy chuckled. "You'd love that, right? Why don't you tell everyone your part in this?"

Lathan put his hands in the air as a sign of surrender. "I'm just the teacher. I only want to help you."

Jeremy jutted his chin upward, glaring at the man. He did step back from the table though, allowing Raleigh to inhale. "Emma texted you that night, too. She wanted to talk to you."

Lathan shook his head, a blank expression. "I don't know what you are talking about."

Raleigh looked at Olivia, who had silent tears running down her face. She looked back at Jeremy and asked. Two very beautiful very young girls. A teacher who had been at the school for at least four years. She looked back at Jeremy and asked, "Was it Emma or Olivia?"

Jeremy fidgeted with the gun. "Emma only wanted to stop Olivia from making a mistake."

The loudspeaker crackled, static bouncing through the stillness of the classroom. "Teachers, we are in lockdown. Hunker down and follow all procedures. I repeat we are in lockdown."

The loudspeaker crackled one more time and then silence descended.

Jeremy raised both hands, the gun pointing toward the ceiling. He began pacing, glaring at each enthralled, terrified face in the room. "You rats. One of you called the office."

He glowered at the room.

"It's not too late," Raleigh said, rushing forward. "Let's just walk out there and explain it all."

Jeremy glared at her a moment, and then shook his head. "Nah, everyone move to that corner." He waved the gun around at the room. "Wait, Dex push that desk in front of the door."

No one moved. All eyes just stared at him.

"Move!" he yelled. Raising the gun toward the back wall of the room, he leveled it with a poster of Einstein's face reading, "A person who never made a mistake never tried anything new." A collective yelp funneled up as a sound equivalent to a popping balloon caused white plaster to blur the air as a lone bullet shattered initial layers of wall.

Trembling teenagers hustled to the back of the room and huddled together, some clutching each other as they whimpered. Serving as a blockade, Mike shepherded the group into a huddled mass and stood between Jeremy and the group. As Olivia rose and stepped backward to join them, Jeremy grabbed her arm and pulled her forward.

Mr. Babin motioned to move toward the corner with Mike, and Jeremy pointed the gun at him. "Not you. I'm not finished with the two of you."

Lathan paused, his eyes darting from Raleigh to Jeremy. Raleigh stepped sideways to even further block his view of the huddled mass.

"Don't do anything you will regret," Raleigh said. "We don't need any of this to discover the truth."

"Oh, yeah?" Jeremy's eyes darkened. "What about my cousin? It's been four years for Courtney, and no one has even bothered looking for the truth. Now Emma? If I let it go, no one will ever know the truth."

Mike held his hand out, motioning downward for calm. "Tell us what you know, and we will make sure the truth comes out."

"You grown-ups are all the same," Jeremy sputtered. "You say that you are listening, but you aren't really. Ask him where he was the night Emma died. Ask him." Jeremy growled as he jerked around, becoming agitated.

Raleigh looked to Lathan. The man's face had paled, and he gazed at the door as if estimating his chances of escape.

Finally, he looked at Raleigh and shook his head in denial. "Look, I don't know what he's talking about. These kids must have cooked something up. You know how teenagers are."

Jeremy chuckled harshly. "Olivia, did you cook something up?"

Tears flowed down Olivia's face. "Why are you picking on me? You're the one that burned Mike's house down. I haven't done anything."

"Because you told me that Mike had been the one with Emma," Jeremy growled. "You have known the truth the entire time, and Emma and Keith are dead because of you."

Olivia's face crumpled as tears spilled over like a rushing dam. "I'm so sorry, but this is not my fault. I never wanted anything to happen to Keith. This is all just so messed up."

Lathan stepped closer to Jeremy and Olivia, staring hard at Olivia. Raleigh didn't miss the coldness in his eyes. "I'm sure you haven't done anything wrong."

Jeremy bucked up and pushed Lathan back with a shove to his chest. "Shut up. You think I don't know what you did?"

Lathan raised his hands in surrender, stepping back. "I just want to help you out. I think you are working on some bad information."

Jeremy smirked. "So you haven't been sleeping with your students?"

Lathan's face flushed and his jaw clenched.

Propped against the back file cabinet, Dex called out, "Come on, man. Banging Olivia isn't the same as murder."

Jeremy sneered down at Olivia. "It is when Emma and Keith threatened to expose Mr. Babin."

Olivia's eyes widened and she gave Lathan an imploring glance, but he wouldn't look away from Jeremy.

Raleigh brushed Olivia's arm. "Why don't you tell us what you know? So, we can help you."

"Help her?" Jeremy grunted. "She caused this."

Mike folded his arms across his chest. "Jeremy, let her speak."

Jeremy glared at Mike but remained quiet.

"Emma wouldn't let it go," Olivia gushed between sobs. "She found out that Lathan and I were..." she glanced at Lathan, whose anger had furrowed his brow and trundled his shoulders. "Anyway, she wouldn't let it go, but it was none of her business." Olivia pleaded as if she wanted them to understand she didn't cause this.

Raleigh held her eye contact with the red head and spoke softly but firmly. "What happened the night Emma died?"

More tears spilled down Olivia's face. "Emma wanted to see me to tell me she had to tell the truth about this, but Lathan said he'd speak to her instead and convince her to keep it quiet."

Raleigh narrowed her eyes, burning into Olivia, who squirmed. "But then how did she end up on Keith's property?"

Sobs raked through her rail-thin petite frame.

Lathan stepped sideways toward the door, his eyes sliding over Raleigh. "I never saw Emma that night. I don't even know how to get to Keith's property. This is a set up."

Raleigh continued to lock eyes with Olivia, whose guilt tore visibly through her.

"I told him where Keith's crawfish ponds were," Olivia sobbed. "Keith and I went there all the time."

"What about Keith?" Mike said. He'd moved in closer, and he and Raleigh exchanged a look.

Olivia shook her head. "I don't know. I felt guilty about Emma and what I knew. I didn't kill her, I swear." Her eyes widened as she looked between Mike and Raleigh. "But Keith... I told him what had happened... he broke up with me..." She gulped. "He said he was going to make sure Lathan paid for what he'd done... but... but... and then he was dead."

Falling to her knees, she sobbed, her body shaking with the admission.

Lathan shook his head, looking down at her with a look of distaste. "You can't prove any of this."

Jeremy waved his arms in the air. "What I can prove is that the bracelet on Emma's body, the bracelet that Courtney had, belonged to your grandmother. She recognized the picture when I showed it to her."

Lathan lunged toward Jeremy, who stumbled backward with the impact of their bodies. As the gun flailed in the air during the struggle, Raleigh dove toward the screaming students and yelled for them to get down.

A loud metal crash followed.

As Raleigh turned, the classroom door swung open and uniformed men with rifles piled in. A stocky gentleman with his cap pulled over his eyes rushed in and tackled the two. As they watched stunned, the officer wrestled the gun away from Jeremy within seconds, who was too dazed to put up much of a fight.

Unencumbered, Lathan stepped back from the SWAT officer, rubbing his chin and shaking his head.

Pointing towards him, Raleigh said, "He murdered the students Emma and Keith."

A young, red-haired SWAT officer, who'd entered the fray after, looked from Raleigh to Lathan. Something in the glance assured him, and he moved in and took Lathan's arm, who shrugged him off at first but then allowed the officer to lead him out of the room.

Jeremy had already disappeared in the chaos.

Raleigh inhaled sharply, feeling a strange panic rise in her.

Then she turned toward Olivia and the other students. Olivia was no longer the only one crying. The two dark-haired student council look-alikes were sobbing, huddled together, rocking each other. Jordan, a heavy set, seven-foot-tall tuba player, slouched against the wall, taking even breaths, his face as red as Luke's hair.

The panic only swirled a moment before it settled. She and Mike exchanged glances and then moved in to offer comfort, providing an arm for security as they escorted them to a chair. The SWAT officer stood guard at the door, but the eleven students could only whisper questions about it being really over in disbelief.

They didn't have to wait for long for an answer. As a crime scene, the investigators wanted to evacuate the premises, but they wanted the students available to give statements. After herding the eleven students into a guidance conference room, Raleigh faced Joey in the hall. The crease across his forehead told her that he'd been worried, but he didn't mention it because he knew she wouldn't like it. Even when they were young, he'd hover over her scraped knees or that broken arm, but she'd have punched him if he'd made a big deal of it. He made a good daddy—just not hers.

Out in the hall surrounded by milling officers, Sheriff Breaux and Max stood together, waiting for the classroom to be cleared for them to go in and do their own walk-through. Several officers around the post minded their posts, and the students had been evacuated already. Raleigh waited to walk them through the scene as instructed, but she wanted to be anywhere she could find chocolate. The hairs on her arms stood on end. The air felt electrified, as if a gun on campus had charged the particles that filled the hallways.

Tapping his boot heavily against the floor, Sheriff Breaux looped his fingers through his belt. "I don't understand why those guys insist on taking so long to secure a room. It's not like we don't have the perpetrator." Glancing in Raleigh's direction, he grunted. "Even though I have to say, I'm disappointed not to have Raleigh Cheramie in handcuffs today." He grinned. "Give it more time, I'm sure it'll happen though."

The officers quieted and their eyes met. Joey's face darkened and his shoulders hunched forward. Raleigh's face burned with anger as well as the emotional draining of the day.

"Sir," Max said, glancing toward Raleigh quickly. "Ms. Cheramie was instrumental in insuring that there was no loss of life in that classroom today. I think we need to give her credit for her actions."

The officers around Raleigh nodded their heads in agreement but didn't glance up from the floor.

Sheriff Breaux looked at Max, his brow furrowed and then back at Raleigh and shook his head. "Can't say I understand how you get all these men under your spell. Is it some kind of voodoo?"

Raleigh frowned. "No, sir. I just practice being a good person."

He rested back on the heel of his boots and glared at her.

His retirement couldn't come soon enough.

TWENTY-FIVE

For the first time since she'd come to Barbeaux Bayou six months ago, Raleigh Cheramie had taken a vacation day. She hadn't even known the correct procedure involved to do this, but David had said he'd handle it for her. She should have possibly taken off and driven to the beach and laid out on the sand until she was red like Leroy's crawfish, but she'd resigned herself to not being wired that way.

"Who are you again?" the petite brunette asked from across the table of the deserted dinner.

Raleigh sighed. "Traiteur to the dead." She offered a smile. "I know that sounds crazy. Folks around here just tend to think I'm crazy or they believe—no in-between."

She nodded slowly, her eyes twitching with a suspicious fear.

"Your mother, Dora, had a message for you," Raleigh said, pushing forward.

The woman leaned forward. "Have you seen her?" she whispered.

Raleigh nodded. "She's watching over your family, and she's worried about your daughter Evie."

"Oh?" The woman shuddered. "Did she tell you this?"

Raleigh drummed her fingers on the sticky metal table of Danny's Po-Boys. "Your mother has her own ideas about how to fix Evie's problems. She wants you—me—to tell your daughter that she's adopted and that's why her stepfather doesn't feel the same way about her."

The woman gasped. "You can't tell my daughter that."

Raleigh sank back in the booth. "I have no plans to do so. What I'm going to tell you is that Evie is hurting herself, and your mother wants to help her. I'm going to allow you to fix it however you want."

"How could you know she's adopted?" the woman mumbled to herself. "No one knows that."

Raleigh sighed. "I don't typically interfere in families. I try to help, but you should help your daughter however you want."

The woman looked up from the table and into Raleigh's eyes. "And my mother wants me to tell my daughter who her real father is?"

Raleigh nodded. "Dora said that the father is sick and doesn't have much longer."

A pained look crumpled in disbelief. "I don't understand how you can know all of this."

Shrugging, Raleigh said, "Dora came to me and asked for my help. I will leave it up to you about helping your daughter though. If your mother is anything like my aunt, she isn't going away no matter what you do."

The woman shook her head. "So you are telling me that my mother's ghost is in my house?"

Ten minutes later, Raleigh had assured Ms. Tammy numerous times that she was only trying to help by delivering a message. When Raleigh left, she felt as though Tammy may have actually believed her about 40 percent.

It didn't matter. Raleigh had made the decision that she needed to begin to listen to the dead, help them tie up their loose ends, and seek their peace.

And after yesterday's events, she needed to plow forward with action.

That's why her next stop on her vacation day was Courtney's house.

After Eula Mae ushered her into the room, Raleigh surveyed the room.

Everything in the living room appeared the same as it had when she and Joey had visited. The curio effigy to her daughter stood intact, drawing Raleigh's attention, even though she attempted to glance the other way. Turning her head away caused her to notice numerous pictures of Courtney on a side table in various sizes and poses.

Eula Mae stood in the front of the sofa and fiddled with the sleeve of her rumpled robe. "Are you sure I can't get you anything?"

Raleigh smiled politely. "No, thank you. I won't keep you long. I just felt as though you deserved some answers about your daughter."

Eula Mae picked at the balled cotton on her robe. "You know Sheriff Breaux won't tell me anything. Says he will in time, but that it would only hurt the case right now."

Raleigh nodded. "Sheriff Breaux is in the middle of a PR nightmare right now with a teacher being responsible."

"I just... I," she stumbled, and then took a deep, haggard breath and pulled her shoulders up under the flimsy robe. "He came to her funeral, you know? All her teachers did four years ago. He sent flowers. I found the card when I heard."

Raleigh exhaled, pushing he uneasiness through her lips. "I thought I'd tell you what I've learned so far and maybe put your mind at ease."

"I don't know if that ever happens," she said bitterly but then motioned for Raleigh to sit. They each took a position on an opposite threadbare sofa. "I do appreciate being told the truth. I've called everyone, and no one is allowed to speak to me."

Raleigh looked at her. Even though her anger had been dulled by grief, it still lay under her words and her thin layer of flesh. "Joey sent me, but he asked me to keep that between us for now."

She leaned back into the sofa and she nodded. "It's nice that someone is looking out for us little folks." She straightened her shoulders. "So how did this happen to my girl?"

Raleigh sighed. "It seems that Courtney became involved with Mr. Babin four months before she died. The chain belonged to Mr. Babin's grandmother, and Courtney took it from him because the relationship was secret, and he wouldn't give her anything."

Eula Mae shook her head, her forehead crinkling. "That doesn't sound like my Courtney."

Raleigh frowned, bracing herself for more objections. "I think the relationship cut her off from all her friends and family, and she started to feel as if she only had Mr. Babin. She began pushing him to plan for their future after high school.

Eula Mae sighed, her eyes downcast as she furiously picked at the cotton balls on her robe.

Raleigh pushed on. "According to Mr. Babin, the two had an argument over the bracelet, and she pushed him, and he put his hand out to hold her off. She tripped and hit her head on the edge of a piling, and he panicked. He thought she was dead."

Eula Mae's lips straightened as her eye twitched. "So he tossed my baby into the canal as if she were old crawfish peelings?"

Raleigh tilted her head in empathy. She couldn't fathom the all-around bad judgment. Joey had said Lathan had proclaimed he'd only been twenty-five and brand new to teaching. He'd defended his poor judgement with youth and hormones, and it made Raleigh's stomach clench in revulsion. "That's his story. He has confessed to Emma and Keith's murder, which were more intentional. He's holding firm on Courtney's being an accident."

Eula Mae shook her head. "It doesn't really matter, does it?"

"No," Raleigh said, "It's still a life gone way too soon."

Eula Mae sat quietly for a moment, staring at a fixed spot above

Raleigh's shoulder, and then her eyes refocused. "Is my daughter at peace?"

As the woman stared at her, Raleigh hesitated. She had no idea what happened once the dying left her with their last moments. But what she did understand was that it wasn't the dying who struggled after the body was found—it was the living.

Raleigh offered a small, reassuring smile. "I believe she is."

Eula Mae nodded, tears glistening and her chin jutting forward as if to deny their spillage. But then her face crumpled.

Later, Raleigh tossed herself on her sofa where Luna's nails tapped against the wood floor, waiting for her attention. Off to install a light fixture at his mom's house, Mike had busied himself this afternoon with wrapping up the arson investigation at his house. Jeremy's confession had at least come with an apology when he'd insisted he didn't know there was a kid in the house, and he would have never if he'd known it wasn't Mike or the kid was in the house. Mike was trying to let it go and helping his mom served as a distraction. Raleigh had the house to herself for a small window of time to enjoy her vacation day. Almost to herself. Luna was an insistent inhabitant and she supposed Aunt Clarice could pop in at any moment uninvited.

Raleigh reached down and picked the puppy up, and she promptly cuddled against Raleigh's chest.

"I guess you aren't so bad."

After recent events, Raleigh supposed her resistance was because the dead didn't strike fear for her anymore, but the living did. They were draining. Maybe between the garden and the puppy, she may be striking some kind of balance.

A knock came at the front door and Luna picked her head up and barked in her high-pitched puppy tone. Not exactly the tone that would scare away the boogeyman.

"Okay girl, let's go see who's here."

Beyond the old wooden French doors, Joey stood with his hat in one hand and a small brown bag in another.

Luna nipped at his tennis shoes, and Joey leaned down and patted the top of the puppy's head.

"Checking in," Joey said.

Motioning for Joey to come inside, Raleigh tried to shepherd the puppy back into the house, but she now ran circles around Joey's feet, over excited at the visitor.

Raleigh threw herself back onto her comfortable sofa, considering the odds of a nap today. "Ms. Eula Mae handled it as well as can be expected. I don't think any of us can understand how Lathan Babin could have done this."

Joey nodded as he sank onto the chair. "Jeremy and Olivia maybe be able to work out plea deals if they agree to testify for the prosecutor. Their lawyers are working on it."

At the end of the day yesterday when all the cards had been laid on the table, Olivia had been brought in and charged with accessory to murder. Raleigh didn't know if she was deserving of the charges, but Sheriff Breaux had made a big to-do in the press conference with the Bayou Blend News program that it was a conspiracy between the two.

Raleigh shrugged. "The girl seemed to know too much about Emma's murder. I'd be careful with her, but I'm not sure I believe she killed them or planned to kill them."

Joey shrugged and scooped up the harried puppy. "It's the DA's case now. Sheriff Breaux has taken it away from me because of your involvement, so I only hear about it when Max or Lieutenant Walter wants to question a statement or get the name of a witness."

"I'm sorry. I keep getting in the way," Raleigh said. There wasn't anything Raleigh could say to make Joey's career trajectory easier in Barbeaux as a Cheramie.

Joey shrugged. "You don't have to be. It's not you." He smiled. "I have decided to run for sheriff. I put my name in, and the wife is getting the signs printed as we speak."

Raleigh felt a surge of excitement. "That's wonderful."

Joey reached into the small brown bag. "Sue Ann had these printed up for you as well."

Accepting the business card he handed her, Raleigh puzzled over the simple, plain white card that read Raleigh Cheramie. Traiteur to the Dead. Her phone number completed the third line. On the back, the card read, *specializing in cold cases for when your loved one's death has unanswered questions.*

Raleigh flipped the card back over, looking up at Joey. "What's this for?"

"Sue Ann thought it was about time for you to begin offering your services. She says you offer something valuable to people, just like Me'Maw."

Tears burned the back of Raleigh's throat as she looked back down at the cards again. Growing up, she'd hoped to be a traiteur like Me'Maw. With Uncle Camille's bitterness, this wouldn't be possible. Maybe this could be her path instead.

Afterall, Paw always said the most important thing in life was to help people.

TWENTY-SIX

Instruments belted out the chords and brassy trumpet of "Before I Grow Too Old" by Tommy McClain, a tune that Me'Maw and Paw had danced to in the kitchen as it played on their old record player. Even though Raleigh knew they had once danced at dance halls, she'd rarely seen these tender moments and had always felt like she was intruding when she watched Paw lead Me'Maw around the kitchen. Now in front of all their friends and family on a makeshift dance floor of old oriental rugs surrounded by a string of light bulbs and wooden folding chairs, the two shuffled about cheek-to-cheek, eyes closed and smiling. Those who weren't watching the happy couple dance milled around the backyard holding paper plates of roasted pig that aromatized the air with its sweet smoky smell.

"You did a great job," Raleigh told Madison as the two clapped to the rhythm of the melody as their parents joined the fray on the dance floor.

"I tried." Madison nodded. "It was actually easier doing it by myself."

"About that," Raleigh said, offering a smile to soften the apology. "Sorry we weren't much help with everything going on."

Nudging her with a thin hip, Madison shook her head with an up curled lip. "It's alright, really. It felt good to be the responsible one for once."

Raleigh laughed. "Oh really?"

"Don't get used to it or anything. It's much easier being me." Madison's expression was completely serious, devoid of humor. They said self-awareness was key, and Madison was nothing if not aware of how selfish she was.

As Raleigh looked around at the Cheramie clan, she caught sight of Uncle Camille sitting in a plastic folding chair far removed from the crowd. From his far-off gaze and stone expression, he didn't appear to be mentally present for the party.

Raleigh nodded in his direction. "I see Uncle Camille made it out of his house?"

Madison rolled her eyes as Mason whizzed by the two of them, jarring sticky, dirty fingers at their face as he passed. "He's up and walking with the power of Budweiser. I lost track at ten or so"

Raleigh raised an eyebrow of disbelief at her sister, and she shrugged.

"At first I tried to stop him, but then I figured he might as well enjoy what time he has left." She shrugged again. "Besides, he's easier to manage when he's not railing at me with all the anger of a dying man. Who placed me in charge of him by the way?"

Raleigh gritted her teeth as she thought about her father and Uncle Jude who'd abandoned him after numerous arguments now. Me'Maw looked to her grandchildren to keep everyone in check. Unfortunately, Uncle Camille held a grudge and wouldn't let Raleigh near him. "Ever notice how family is only close when they want something but not when something needs to be done?"

Madison nodded. "Until the glue is gone and then we don't have to worry about it anymore."

Coldness spread through her as she watched Me'Maw and Paw dance. She felt death in the air. A tingle of ashes and dirt in her nose.

She'd lose someone here soon. She felt it in her bones. She swallowed against the panic of it.

Approaching the table that Madison and Raleigh stood behind, Mike held out a single white daisy.

He grinned, his dimple forming. "It's time for our date."

The tables held vases of daisy sprigs, so Raleigh tried to calm her erratic heartbeat and dismissed the gesture as his plucking a flower from the table.

Raleigh laughed, a forced sound to her ears as she attempted to calm herself. "We are in the middle of a party."

Mike held out his hand. "I know. We aren't going far."

Raleigh glanced toward Madison, who wore a conspiratorial smile. The two had planned something. Her heart fluttered.

Raleigh accepted Mike's outreached hand and allowed him to lead her away from the overloaded food tables and past the dance floor, past the mingling groups talking about how things were forty years ago. The two walked along the old cypress barn, and Raleigh felt only the cool shade of the building and not the death that she'd once felt crawling around its insides. Her heart began to feel lighter.

They turned the corner behind the barn where a small bistro table awaited them. Arranged plates of pulled pork sandwiches and Aunt Lydia's potato salad sat waiting under full arrangements of potted daisies.

Taking in the folded yellow napkins and a stack of Twix bars on a cake plate, Raleigh looked to Mike expecting a hidden joke. "You did all of this?"

Grinning, Mike motioned for her to take the seat he now stood behind. "I thought we have waited long enough for our first date, and your grandparent's anniversary may offer us a little bit of luck, if you believe in that sort of thing."

Sinking into the seat, Raleigh noticed an old, dingy, white Hot Wheels racecar on the table. Scratches cut across the sides and the peeling number 8 sticker on the doors looked as if it had bumped into many walls in its glory days of play. As Mike took the seat across from her, Raleigh picked up the car, remembering the headlights and black tires.

"You kept this?" Raleigh asked, trying to remember how long ago they'd played with this particular car every day.

Mike nodded, his fingers bouncing on the tablecloth. "My mom kept it. Remember how we played with this car every day at recess in kindergarten, and we'd take turns taking it home each night?"

Raleigh smiled. She remembered the times they'd send it flying with those black wheels spinning from the top of the monkey bars just to test how far they could launch it on the playground. This one car had entertained them every day the entire school year.

Spinning the wheels, Raleigh asked, "Why did you keep it?"

Mike smiled. "In kindergarten, I had such a crush on you. I couldn't wait to see you every day with those awful jagged bangs and brown boots. You'd shout and get excited over those fifteen minutes we'd get to run around and fly a car, not like the other girls who wanted to play jump rope or just walk around talking. What did we know about love?" Mike chuckled. "Or did we know everything we needed to know back then? Because at the end of kindergarten, I thought we could be friends forever instead. You were cooler than the other girls, and you were Ree, you know? The one always coming up with something cool to try. It would be just the two of us forever."

Raleigh's eyes watered as she felt the truth of his words. She and Mike had known each other since they were four years old. She'd known the boy and now the man. Every story—memory—of her life had Mike wrapped in its crevices. It had always been him.

Mike took her hand, holding the car inside of their palms together. "I'm still that five-year-old with a crush, but we can't keep waiting for a next chance because a person only gets so many chances."

"Are you certain that you are ready for seriousness? I mean your record is three dates, and my record is a broken engagement and broken relationships," Raleigh said.

Mike nodded, squeezing her hand gently. "Yes, and I know we can be both friend and a crush. We can have the best of both worlds."

Raleigh nodded. For the first time, she felt it too.

ACKNOWLEDGMENTS

Though this story takes place in a fictional world, it is a conglomerate of the places of my childhood memories. I consult the people around me continuously to keep the perspective of South Louisiana. I also want to thank those who offered stories and help along the way in keeping the Cajun aspects authentic.

ALSO BY JESSICA TASTET

The Raleigh Cheramie Series

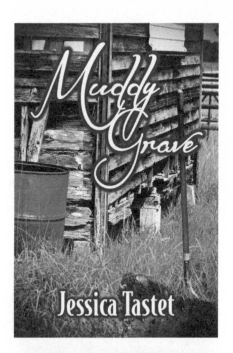

Muddy Grave

Jessica Tastet

MUDDY HEARTS

Jessica Tastet

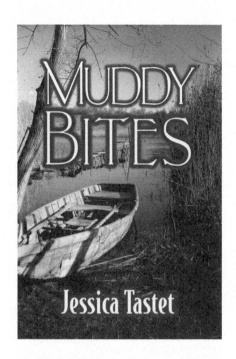

The Treasure Trilogy

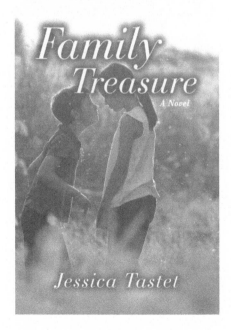

Coming Soon.... *Borrowed Treasure*

THE CUSTOS SAGA

ABOUT THE AUTHOR

JESSICA TASTET is the author of six novels and a children's story. She's worked in education for twenty-two years and as an editor for six years. She lives in Louisiana with her family.

For updates visit:
www.jessicatastet.com